GLADWIN COUNTY
402 JAMES RO
GLADWIN
"Serving and preserving since 1954"

Fated

SHILOH WALKER

ELLORA'S CAVE
ROMANTICA PUBLISHING

What the critics are saying...

❧

DRAGON'S WARRIOR

5 Angels "This reviewer found the book a fantastical odyssey. [...] Totally immersed in this story, there was no way to put it down until the end was reached. [...] Shiloh Walker may be new to the romance scene but she is blazing a trail to reach many readers with her insightful plots and fantastical stories. She is definitely an author of extreme talents that many eager readers will be anticipating each new release anxiously." ~ *Fallen Angels Reviews*

DRAGON'S WOMAN

4 Rating "Set in a world filled with diverse magical creatures, *The Dragon's Woman* is an exciting and enthralling read. [...] When things started to go wrong he was bewildered as to what he'd done wrong let alone how to fix it; dealing with emotions was not something natural for his species and occasionally Eilrah behaved as a child but his reactions to Rianne were anything but childish. Rianne was strong when she needed to be but showed an entrancing vulnerability that created a fascinatingly complex character. [...] *The Dragon's Warrior* will defiantly be enchanted with Ms Walker newest tale *The Dragon's Woman*. I look forward to reading more stories set in this multi faceted world in the future." ~ *Erotic-Escapades Reviews*

An Ellora's Cave Romantica Publication

www.ellorascave.com

Fated

ISBN 9781419957758
ALL RIGHTS RESERVED.
Dragon's Warrior Copyright © 2003 Shiloh Walker
Dragon's Woman Copyright © 2006 Shiloh Walker
Edited by Pamela Campbell.
Cover art by Syneca.

This book printed in the U.S.A. by Jasmine–Jade Enterprises, LLC.

Trade paperback Publication May 2008

With the exception of quotes used in reviews, this book may not be reproduced or used in whole or in part by any means existing without written permission from the publisher, Ellora's Cave Publishing, Inc.® 1056 Home Avenue, Akron OH 44310-3502.

Warning: The unauthorized reproduction or distribution of this copyrighted work is illegal. Criminal copyright infringement, including infringement without monetary gain, is investigated by the FBI and is punishable by up to 5 years in federal prison and a fine of $250,000.
(http://www.fbi.gov/ipr/)

This book is a work of fiction and any resemblance to persons, living or dead, or places, events or locales is purely coincidental. The characters are productions of the author's imagination and used fictitiously.

JAN 19 2010

FATED

ൟ

DRAGON'S WARRIOR
~11~

DRAGON'S WOMAN
~141~

DRAGON'S WARRIOR

ଓ

Chapter One

ಬಾ

Kye went from hovering beside the headstone while Connor and Ashlyn stood over it, straight into nothingness. Where he drifted for what felt like eons, in a fog that had no shape, no color, no scent. Where he was just an insubstantial thought, with no body—just his memories.

And anger.

Impotent rage and immeasurable frustration.

Is this what he had hurried to? The reason he had told her she needed to let him go?

Had he left her for this? To just hover in this nothingness? Kye had been expecting—well, *something*. Granted, he may not have been good enough for heaven, and he certainly wasn't looking forward to hell. But just to linger here in this limbo seemed worse than hell.

Maybe it was hell. This lack of everything. Hadn't he heard once that a baby could die from lack of stimulus? No color other than the gray that surrounded him, no sounds, no scents, no touch.

It was certainly enough to drive a person insane.

And right when he was getting really pissed, he was thrown into a well of pain. Maybe *this* was hell—this intense, excruciating pain. Sharp biting teeth worked over his body, and icy winds blew right through him. A strange, burning scent filled his nostrils and the air he breathed burned and scorched his lungs. Bright lights pierced his eyes and his naked flesh felt cold. Was he being born?

And then he was thrown back into that odd void where he could see and listen but never talk or touch.

Only it wasn't his world. And it wasn't Ashlyn he was watching.

It was a long, leggy brunette with firm, large tits and a tight little ass that made his mouth water and his cock stand at attention. When she went down on all fours, he could see her tightly puckered rosette and he wondered if she had ever taken a man's cock in her rear.

Right now she was taking one down her throat, and obviously enjoying every single second of it. Long slim fingers were busily stroking her clit while she suckled and licked at the large cock of her partner. Once more, he was separated from everything by a wall, but he could see, and hear, and smell. Her cream had her fingers gleaming and the air was perfumed by her body and her lust.

Bizarrely enough, it was something else that kept catching his eye. An odd necklace. Maybe amulet was a better word. It hung from a chain of hammered silver, darkened as if with age. The stone was the size of a baby's fist and looked cloudy and dull.

He tore his gaze back to the woman as she turned and presented her rump to her lover, gazing at him with hot, teasing eyes as she spread her thighs, opening her folds more, cream starting to drip down her thighs.

Kye wasn't even aware he was moving until he was kneeling in front of her, staring once more at the amulet that swung between her lovely breasts. A dull roaring noise filled his ears, drowning the moans and cries, while he stared into that stone.

He yelped and fell backward onto his ass.

The stone had cleared, for just a moment. And it had reflected his face.

And then Kye was drifting, just as she started to take her partner's length inside. One second he was there, watching— then drifting.

Next he saw them busily fucking on a cloth thrown on the ground beside a waterfall. He felt the aching, heavy sensation of his engorged cock and, after freeing it from his jeans, he grasped it, stroked, knowing the climax wasn't going to come.

That damned stone hanging around her neck kept drawing his eyes. It started to glow, subtly, while they fucked. Kye was moving closer, whether to see them more clearly, or to see the stone, he didn't know.

And he was sucked back out of reality and left there for what seemed like an age.

And then a new girl, a smaller, rougher version of the first was sucking down the man's cock, playing with his furred sac, flirting with his anus, while he ate at his lady's cream drenched vagina, snaking his long tongue inside her, smacking at the side of her ass as she screamed in release. She looked different now, a little older, maybe nineteen or twenty. The breasts that framed the necklace were fuller and even more perfect.

Kye settled back on his heels, watching with hunger as the man mounted her and shoved his shaft inside her, plowing deep while he took her mouth in a series of rough biting kisses.

Then Kye was gone again.

When he came back into reality, they were standing upright against a wall, her long lean thighs clamped around her partner's waist while he rode her hard. Kye could hear her screaming and moaning, hear the smack of flesh against flesh, and smell the sweat that dewed their bodies. The stone was really glowing now and her eyes were almost reflecting the light, the warm brown depths gleaming an odd, reddish gold hue.

On the hearth, an odd cat-like creature lay, watching the show with faintly disgusted eyes before he resumed grooming his long, pale blue coat of fur.

It was oddly quiet, save for the sounds of their fucking. Her long, rough moan filled the air, followed by a murmur of exotic words against the man's throat. He lowered his head to kiss her deeply as he released her body to the floor, the tenderness in that kiss making the ache in Kye's heart double.

Ash, baby, I miss you, he thought, rubbing his aching chest with the heel of his hand.

Chapter Two

ॐ

Suddenly he was sucked back into limbo—then thrown right back—only to hear the sounds of petrified screams. When Kye could actually see again, he could see the girl trying desperately to close the gaping neck wound of her lover. But his eyes were blank and empty, dead. Dark crimson blood had dried on his neck and the floor beneath him.

Big, cruel hands tore the amulet away and a rough, archaic looking hammer smashed the stone. When that happened, Kye watched as her back arched with pain and she screamed long and loud, her eyes glassy and half wild.

She was torn from her lover's side and gagged, tied, thrown roughly over a man's shoulder and taken into the wild, deep woods that surrounded the small village.

The cat-like creature lay outside the gates, his head smashed. Next to him was the mutilated and raped body of the second girl.

Kye stood in numb shock, in horror—then he started battering the barrier that kept him from getting too close. Over and over, until he fell back into limbo with a muttered curse on his lips, his body aching from his useless war against the barrier.

When he returned, they were cutting her long black hair, laughing at the outrage and humiliation in her eyes. Then they oiled her head and shaved off the short locks that remained, until her scalp gleamed naked and pale in the firelight.

Kye's throat hurt from bellowing, and his fists hurt from pounding on the barrier. Nausea, hot and sour, roiled in his gut, but even the option of puking and ridding himself of this vile feeling was gone. He bellowed out when the men threw her nubile young body to the ground and molested her.

And always, always, after a few minutes, he was sucked back into limbo. Weeks, maybe months passed. He kept track of time by how long he had been gone, by how long her ebony hair had grown since he had seen her last, how many bruises had faded, and how many new ones appeared to take their place.

By day, the two men who had taken her traveled at a merciless pace, sometimes carrying her, sometimes dragging her along behind them. They beat her, molested her, and kept her bound and gagged. The gag only came off when they had had to force feed and hydrate her to keep her alive.

"What's going on?" Kye whispered, trying to close his eyes against the horror of them fondling her, beating her.

Her hair had grown probably half an inch before they shaved it off again. That same night, they started to tend to her myriad bruises and cuts. That same night, when she spat food in their faces, they didn't retaliate.

And that had a sickening fear growing in his belly.

They traveled north, until they left behind the woods for cold gray mountains, higher and higher, until they reached a solid stone fortress.

Inside the stone fortress, he followed, unable to keep more than four or five yards distance between his 'body' and hers. Each time he lagged, he was pulled forward, shoved forward, dragged, by some unseen presence.

So he watched, helplessly, while they tied her weakened body to a stone table, her legs spread wide, her hands tied beneath her at an uncomfortable angle. Watched while they ordered a slim young blonde woman, clad only in a metal collar, to trim her pubic hair and wax her mound, until she was bare and gleaming from the oil that had been used to soothe her reddened flesh.

One of the jailors threw the young blonde to the ground, mounted her struggling body roughly and raped her while the other went and slid his fingers over the listless woman's naked mound and inside her vagina, while he jacked off with his free hand, and laughed at the revulsion in her eyes.

When he spewed her in the face with his semen, Kye shot to his feet and swung out, feeling a snap, deep inside his hand, and hearing a reverberating pop. It vibrated, in his mind, in his chest, in the air that surrounded them. The men beyond the barrier had paled, each pulling away and covering suddenly flaccid cocks, eyes wildly searching.

The air around them still shuddered and the rage inside Kye seemed to leak out and fill the room, filling it with rage and a promise of retribution.

A feral smile curved Kye's mouth and he sank back down to his heels, watching.

They had heard him.

The barrier was growing thin.

So he watched as they scurried away, and waited.

As he rose some time later, he could feel himself falling again.

Back into the pain. Into the brutal biting teeth that tried to tear his flesh from his bones, back into the blistering cold winds, the painfully bright lights that stung his eyes and made them water. The air was permeated with a burning, scorching smell, and it nearly choked him as he fell into sleep.

* * * * *

And then he woke up.

From nothingness into this.

Maybe he was dreaming. Maybe he hadn't been hit by that car and this was all a bizarre dream. Or maybe that car had really hit him and he was in a deep coma. Did coma victims dream?

But he wasn't dreaming.

Opening his eyes, he stared into a lilac sky, a lilac he had only rarely seen in an unusual sunset at home.

And since the sun shining in his eyes was what had woken him, he knew twilight was nowhere close.

Cautiously, he rose. And rose. And rose. Until he was standing fully upright, a good foot and half taller than he should have been, his body longer and paler and scarred. And, surprise, surprise, completely nude. He lifted shaking hands in front of his face and stared at the wide large palms, the fine reddish gold hair sprinkled on the backs. He drove those unfamiliar hands through his hair, receiving another shock when he felt, then saw the dark red locks. As curly as Ashlyn's had been after she'd had a loose spiral perm put in her hair. It was a deep, dark, pure red, darker than Ashlyn's, a deep burgundy-red.

With a glance down, he confirmed everything else was different. Instead of an average seven-inch cock, he had a good ten inches. Instead of narrow, rather small feet, he had long, narrow feet. Instead of a pale golden hue, his skin was winter white and rippling with corded muscles.

"What the fuck..." he whispered. Then he cocked his head. A familiar voice.

"*Orinduuc.*"

"*Orinducc.*"

A weak, desperate whisper. "Come to me. Bound we are, you are mine to come. Dragon I call you—dragon, I summon you. Come. *Orinduuc.*"

Then the voice was muffled, followed by a vicious slapping sound, the sound of a body tumbling to the ground. Apparently, his hearing was much improved as well as everything else, Kye decided, as he started jogging down the faint game trail along the tall stone wall. He dove through a narrow opening in the brush that opened to a tiny gate. And how had he known that was there?

Watching through the metal slats, concealing his large, naked body behind the thicket, he watched as the girl was dragged down the path and back inside the fortress. "Stupid bitch! I'll kill Miara for letting her loose," a guard muttered, staring at the sky in fear. Searching. For what?

How had he understood them? "What in the fuck is going on? What am I doing here?" he muttered. He hadn't expected an answer.

And he never expected what it was that gave the answer.

"There was a...mix-up," a deep, gruff, *large* voice said from behind.

Slowly, Kye turned.

And looked up. And up. And up. Into glowing, deep red eyes—eyes that looked like the stone the girl had worn around her neck. He looked into those eyes, trying to understand what he was seeing.

It looked like, well, a dragon. Covered with green and gold and purple scales and a good twenty feet long, crouched there on the game trail, the trees seeming to bend out of his way as he edged closer. The scales grew smaller and darker colored along the length of his snakelike neck. By the time the scales touched his large triangular head—roughly the size of a compact car—they were deep, deep crimson, his eyes almost blending into the glittering scales.

"I'm nuts. That's the explanation," Kye muttered.

A dragon.

He swore when he realized he hadn't spoken in English. He had spoken in that lyrical tongue that the girl had spoken in. The tongue he had understood.

"What in the hell is going on? Where am I?" he demanded, striding naked out of the brush, to glare at the dragon that could eat him in one big bite.

"There was a mix up," the dragon repeated. "You weren't supposed to be born where you were born. This was supposed to be your reality." With a sigh, he settled his triangular head on his foreclaws and studied Kye.

"You were supposed to be born here, and Connor was supposed to be born into your body, the one they buried. Of course, he's with Ashlyn, which is what was supposed to happen. So not everything was destroyed. And when you ah, died, we brought you here."

"We?" Kye repeated, keeping his voice low. Part of him knew this was to keep them from discovery — although how a huge red and gold dragon with a ruby-red head and eyes that glittered like jewels hadn't been discovered confounded him. The other part was blathering in confusion, wondering how the first part had known to speak low and quiet.

"Mmm. Eiona was to be yours."

Eiona. Eiona.

The girl.

And suddenly, other memories that weren't his were in his mind. And he was being trained.

To be a warrior.

A lover.

A protector.

Taking up a sword when he was still a child, to bring down a wild oxiat that had ravaged his mother's village. Being taken into a priest's home to learn magic, into a harem to learn, at a young age the feel of a woman's flesh — how to take his pleasure and how to give hers.

The sword. The sword.

It was in his hand.

He didn't even know how it had come to be there, but he was holding it, four something feet of long, deadly, razor sharp metal that gleamed an odd blue under the midday sun. Scrolled markings that should have tricked his eyes were clear and easy to read. "*Aldrian-elai.* Warrior-maker." Kye raised glittering eyes to the dragon, eying him over the expanse of metal. "A sword doesn't make a warrior."

"No. The warrior will make the sword. There's magic in that blade, magic that can help you." He nodded to the pile of cloth at his feet. It lay alongside a long wooden bow and a quiver of arrows, five different knife sheathes, a short throwing axe, a garrote. "You may want to dress. That white hide of yours will catch the eye, sooner or later."

As he donned the clothes, he studied the weapons. And he knew he could use them. He knew where they went, knew how to conceal them, how to bring them out quickly.

The memories were there. But they weren't his.

And his other memories, the ones that were really his, were fading. A compu-tech sounded foreign. And he could barely bring Ashlyn's face to mind.

"Ashlyn," he whispered, forcing the words out in English. "Why can't I see her face?"

"Because she is fading from you," the dragon said softly, watching him with alien eyes. "Soon, you will forget all but the memories that should have been yours."

"I'd rather die," Kye rasped. Forget her? Forget his life?

"Then so will Eiona. You are her protector. If you do not save her, no one will," the dragon said.

Eiona.

"This is insane," Kye insisted.

"This is reality, and you know it. I speak only the truth," the dragon returned, raising his head and glaring down at the human before him. "You are her protector."

"I don't know how to be a protector," Kye argued futilely, his mind wheeling in frantic circles. Eiona, die? Him a protector? And Ashlyn. Even if his mind was letting her go — his heart, his body — remembered her. "I am *not* a warrior. I don't know how to be a warrior."

"You do know."

Kye lifted his hands in front of his face, discovered they were shaking. What was going on?

Lifting narrowed eyes to the dragon, he whispered, "Talk."

The body had belonged to a man called Rue, and he had been training since birth to take his place at Eiona's side. To be her protector, her strength. To be her lover.

To be hers. Her *elai*. The word alone meant more than just warrior. Only the warrior who had been promised to the priestess was *elai*. Her warrior. Her lover. Her center.

But the man Rue had been a mistake as well. Born into the wrong line, born into the wrong body. A cruel man, placed in a position of great worth, great power. A dangerous combination.

"Rue cared for little but himself. He was cruel, selfish and pitiless. And pitiful. Rue developed a taste for the *quaite*, a powder that brings strength, stamina and virility. And eventually, death. A slow, addictive poison."

Kye was slammed back into a body, or back in time, and felt his heart slowing in his chest, felt his breath stop in his lungs, felt himself die. Then he watched, from the outside, as a pale sickly light rose slightly from the body and evaporated into thin air.

Watched as another came careening in, smashing into the body with such force it cause the body to flinch. The graying cast that had been spreading over the corpse faded, replaced by a soft, gentle golden glow.

"Oh, he didn't die. Or, well, he wouldn't have, yet. If I hadn't helped him along. But you needed your body. This body, the one you should have been born into. So I speeded the process."

Speeded the process.

It sounded so clinical.

This lizard had snatched him from his body before his spirit could fade. And then he shoved him into this one. With a side-trip along the way. "Why the field trip? I spent six fucking months watching Ashlyn suffer through the days. What was the point?"

"Letting her go. Knowing she would be fine," the dragon replied. "Otherwise, in your soul, you would have been uneasy. Although she wasn't your life mate, she was your heart. She held your heart for a long time. You had to know she was going to be well without you."

With a muttered, "Fuck," Kye shot to his feet, pacing the tiny path. "I don't believe in this. I can't believe this. I don't want this life. I want *my* life. The one I was born into, the body I was born into."

The dragon sighed, lowered his huge head. "I can't do that. I am no god. No divine being. I am an avatar, of sorts. I can guide, instruct and teach. But I cannot change the past. And your other life is past. It is over. It will fade. Your body is turning to dust in the ground, and your woman has fallen in love with another man."

Kye's eyes narrowed and his fists clenched. A red wash of fury washed in front of him and he growled, "How nice of you to remind me, you overgrown lizard."

"Watch yourself, mortal."

"Watch this, you stupid fuck," Kye hissed, dropping the hilt of his sword to the ground and preparing to throw his body on it. There was an edginess in his head, in his soul, something that didn't feel quite like himself and the pain in his heart was riding him, driving him nearly insane. Live in this world? Alone? In this alien place where nothing made sense to him? Without Ashlyn?

"So easy to let an innocent woman die? When you can save her?"

Wearily, Kye dropped to his knees, the sword falling across his lap. The soft dark brown leather on his leg blended with the dark, decaying foliage on the ground. "What are you? Who are you?"

"Your shield-brother. I am hers, her *Orinduuc*. Born to serve and protect her, as were you."

"Then why don't you save her?"

"She hasn't learned how to call me yet."

Then, while Kye stared with disbelieving eyes, the dragon faded away, first into a sheer form, then an insubstantial mist, leaving nothing but a fading, glittery fog.

Chapter Three

ஐ

Eiona had finally worked her hands free of the ropes binding her. It had been damn near impossible, with her arms tied as they were. But finally, finally the ropes had loosened as she sat up slowly, her aching, abused body reluctant to move, even with the possibility of freedom only yards away.

She rubbed and massaged her palms a moment, forcing them to move the way they should before she reached for the ropes at her ankles.

She had a chance if she could get outside.

She had been close.

She had felt the magic flowing inside her, like a dam ready to break free. If her focus stone hadn't been shattered all those months ago, she would have succeeded before now. The magic was there and it was ready. But she couldn't get centered to call it.

If she could only get back outside, feel the earth beneath her feet, the wind on her face. She might be able to do it, even without her focus.

And the power of the *Oriniic,* the homeland, flowing through from so many miles away. She was *Orin* – a priestess of the Earth, a fey spirit inside a mortal body.

And she could call her *Orinduuc.*

She used her bindings, tying them into one longer awkward rope. It would hold. It only had to lower her three or four lengths. If she had been in better form, she could have jumped it easily.

But she was weak.

After wedging a hefty chair against the door, she secured her rope and straddled the window, gasping as the bare stone chafed against her bare groin. Her skin still stung slightly from the waxing and her naked flesh made her feel even more exposed.

The bastards.

She clambered down the makeshift rope as quickly as she could, caring little how much noise she made. The men they had put on her were strong and quick, but not terribly bright.

If they had been bright, they would have chained her in a dungeon, away from the air, the sunlight, all the things that fed her strength. Skinny as she had become, she was in no real danger. Just setting bare feet on the ground below her steadied her. If she were given the time, the energies from the earth would flow through her—ease her pain, calm her fears, and heal her body.

And if she were successful, she would have that time.

Soon.

She had his name now. It had come to her as they dragged her away from the open air the last time she had tried to call him. *Orinduuc* was what he was to her, but his name was Eilrah.

"Eilrah."

"Eilrah."

"Eilrah."

"Eilrah."

This time, as she spoke, her voice grew firmer. She could do this. She could finally summon the *Orinduuc*. The doubt that had plagued her for months now finally lifted. She could do this. Lifting her face to the sun, her arms spread high overhead, she felt the wind caress her nude body as she called out in a high, clear voice, "Come to me. Bound we are, you are mine to come. Eilrah, come. Eilrah, I bid you, come to me, *now!*"

"Emid, the bitch has gotten outside!" the smaller of the guards was shouting.

Emid replied savagely, "Shut her up, or we all die, you fool."

She heard the muffled shouts and bellows of her captors, but stood firm, feeling a rushing gale from inside her body, feeling the blood that seemed to pulse hotter and faster inside her veins.

And the magic that pulsed in the air around her.

Then magic exploded, and out of the nebulous of that explosion, a large shape started to take form. Huge, glittering wings of black, edged with dark gold and green, his ruby red body shot through with scales of violet, of green and of gold. Spines of pure ebony marching down a long snake like neck and mammoth body. His huge spear-shaped head was the color of a ruby threaded with gold, each scale a deep, glimmering red, edged with gold.

He was beautiful.

Eilrah.

A deep roar echoed through the air as the dragon surged out of the nebulous, crossing from his plane to hers in one giant leap. By the time her captors tumbled out of the house, Eilrah stood before her, one foreleg drawn up to his chest, his wings spread wide.

One of the men turned and ran.

But the other ran for her. Weak as she was, Eiona was unable to move quickly enough as he pinned her against the stone wall, with his sword at her neck. "Make one move, dragon, and we will see what color the blood of a priestess flows," he panted, staring at the towering giant, his blade pressed deep, deep into her flesh, already drawing blood. Eiona could feel it running warm and wet down her neck.

"I doubt that."

The man froze.

That was a new voice. Or rather, a voice Eiona hadn't heard in ages. She had truly hoped to never hear it again.

But Rue stood behind the man, his blade already at the smaller man's neck, his forearm gripping him tight. "Let her go. Or I'm going to break your fucking neck," Rue whispered harshly, his eyes never once looking her way.

Eiona took a gasping breath as the blade fell away. She stumbled forward, away from them. Forward, until she could collapse at Eilrah's feet. A strange rustling sound filled the air and then one wing, much smaller now, folded over her bare shoulders. He crooned to her in dragon tongue, a soft, strange murmuring lullaby as Rue faced her captor over the length of his blade.

Aldrian-elai. The blade gleamed in the fading twilight, a soft, eerie blue and silver light that illuminated his opponent's face, which was stark, blank.

The face of a man who knew he was going to die.

Rue released his hold slowly and walked around Emid, still holding the blade at the man's throat, his dark eyes narrow, hot, angry. That was rather, well, odd. Eiona had never known Rue to be angry over anybody's misfortune other than his own.

"Why did you take her?"

Eiona started, her eyes flying to Rue's face. An odd question, surely. Emid's eyes narrowed and he laughed. "Don't you know why? The Sorcerer wants her. Her body. Her blood. Her magic. It's so rare to find a priestess who hasn't tapped into it yet.

"Alas. Too late now," the man said, his eyes briefly flitting to Eilrah. "He'll settle for her body and blood, I imagine." The sorcerer. Nobody knew who he really was, only that young witches and priestesses ended up dead under his hands. He had been destroying the women in the land for decades and they still hadn't found him after all this time.

"Her blood and body would be enough for what he has in mind, I would say," Eilrah growled, his long tongue snaking out the taste the air around Emid. "Where is he?"

Emid laughed. "Coming," was all he would say though. And after he said it, he ran forward screaming.

And impaled his body along the length of *Aldrian-elai*. Rue staggered slightly, his eyes wide and shocked.

Shocked. That wasn't a look she tended to associate with Rue. He was a bastard, a user, a snake unworthy of his calling. And far too jaded to ever be shocked.

Of course, it wasn't exactly like Rue to come after her. Rue would have raised a mug of ale in toast to the bastards who had taken her, probably taken Aiken's fallen body and skinned it, cured it and used it as a rug in front of his fire. Rue was no hero.

Although he had been meant to be.

And that infuriated Eiona. Had from the very beginning. From infancy, she had always known she was bound to Rue. She had intended to honor that binding. Had looked to that day with yearning.

And then she had met him. Oh, he had been handsome— that long, pale body, so strong, his deep-red hair flowing long and free to his shoulders. Those large, dark eyes, his full sculpted mouth.

Handsome? Damnation, yes.

Nearly a prefect male, his body marred with a warrior's scars. Sexual, sensual, and promised to her.

And his soul so tainted.

Three years past, she had met him. He had sickened and frightened her. The naked lust in his eyes, the cruelty she glimpsed in his face, his hard, uncaring hands when he had followed her into her dwelling. He had pinned her to the wall, rubbed his cock against her and laughed when she wriggled and shoved at him.

"Get used to it, little priestess. You belong to me," he had rasped while he palmed her breast and shoved himself between her thighs.

That was also the day she had sworn she would never join with her *elai*. While one day she had known he would come to serve at her side, she had sworn never to serve at his. She may have to suffer his presence while she attended her duties; but she wouldn't suffer it at night.

It wasn't long after that she had met Aiken.

She keened softly under her breath, mourning him.

Her head fell forward and she rested her brow on the ground, crying softly, a high lilting chant falling from her lips as she wished her fallen lover a swift crossing into the next life.

And wished she had taken Rue. If she had taken him, maybe it would be his body lying cold and lifeless in a stone tomb back in the *Oriniic*. Rue, not Aiken.

Something warm and sweet smelling covered her body. It smelled of cedar and vanilla. Strong, warm arms lifted her and she knew she was being carried.

Distantly, she heard Rue and Eilrah speaking. But she didn't care what they were saying. She cared for little save that she was alive, Aiken was dead, and she was alone.

Kye sat at the fire, his back against a rough stone wall, his long legs sprawled out in front him. He studied the hands he held in front of his face, rubbing one palm against the other, fingering a ridge of scar tissue. Closing his eyes, he summoned Ashlyn's face out of his memories.

He had discovered that if he tried to focus on what she had made him feel, on the love they had shared, it was easier to bring an image of her to mind. Sweet, laughing Ashlyn. He could remember them fucking on twisted sheets while the moon shone through the window, to bathe their bodies in silvery light. Remember how it had felt when she would straddle him and ride his cock while she stroked and pinched her nipples, laughing and pulling out of reach when he tried to touch her.

He snarled at the images in his head when they twisted until it was Connor he saw in his memories—Connor watching as she walked down the aisle dressed in ivory lace and silk, Connor fucking his wife while Kye was kept away by the damned barrier.

"Stop it," he growled, his eyes flying open and pinning Eilrah. "Stop it. They are my memories, *mine*. And you don't have any right to be toying with them."

Eiona had been dozing in the corner—exhausted by her ordeal—but when he spoke, her eyes flew open. "I do nothing..."

"This helps you little. Why torture yourself, human?"

"Because I am human, you stupid lizard, and humans love to torture themselves. It's also my mind, my memories and you've no say over them." He shoved to his feet and glared over the fire at the lounging dragon. Who, right now, was roughly the size of a Clydesdale. Large, yes. But not as intimidating as he had been when he was roughly the size of a school bus, excluding the wings. Kye was forcing his thoughts into what he knew was normal, even though thinking of Clydesdales and school buses felt foreign.

The more he thought like he used to think, the easier it was. The less foreign it felt. Which made him think that forgetting wasn't something that would have happened on its own. It was being helped.

"Smart one, aren't you?" Eilrah said with a deep, rumbling bass of a laugh. Who was that actor...stocky, round black guy with the deep voice. Ah, James Earl Jones. He sounded like James Earl Jones.

"Smart enough to figure out when some one is playing tricks with my mind," he snapped.

"Do not speak to him," Eiona commanded, sitting up. The loose cottony shirt Kye had put on her swallowed her. The neck fell off one shoulder to lie beguilingly over one naked breast.

"I'll speak to whomever the hell I wish," Kye replied, glaring at her. Only to realize she wasn't speaking to him.

"You are not supposed to be able to communicate with him," Eiona said, rising from her nest of blankets to stare at Eilrah. "How is this possible?"

"I can speak to whomever I choose, little one," Eilrah said, cocking his head to study her.

"And you chose to speak to *him*? He is not worthy of speaking to you. Have you any idea what kind of bastard he is?" she shrieked, waving one hand in Kye's direction.

Kye leaned one shoulder against the cave wall, watching with raised eyebrows. He had just saved that ungrateful little brat's hide. Granted, he wasn't quite sure how a fight between him and a true warrior would have turned out, but, hell, didn't he deserve credit for trying?

"Be careful, little one," Eilrah said, moving until he could place his snout directly in her lovely, angry face. "Things are not always as they seem."

"Oh, so he is truly a good man; he was just pretending to molest me when I was barely fifteen. Just pretending to hurt all the women I've heard stories about."

Eilrah huffed, streams of smoke blowing out his nostrils. "He's not the man you knew, little one."

"Why don't you tell her the story you handed me, lizard?" Kye asked, pretending to study his nails. Buffing the short, clipped nails against his leather jerkin, he grinned. "Think she'll believe it any better than I did?"

"Watch how you to speak to my *Orinduuc*, you pathetic piece of slime," she hissed, turning to glare at him.

"Or what? You'll turn me into a toad? Or crush my heart? Turn me into stone?" he offered helpfully while Eilrah closed his eyes in the background and prayed for patience.

"A toad? Why would I turn you into a toad? *How* could I turn you into a toad?" she said, her eyes narrowed. "Of course, crushing your heart, if you had one, sounds rather promising."

If the pure venom in her eyes was anything to go by, she was serious. Kye laughed. Dropping down on his single blanket, he mused what an interesting day it had been. His first day in flesh in what seemed like ages.

"I'm not done talking to you, *elai*."

"I'm done taking orders from you, priestess," he said, closing his eyes and sighing happily when Ashlyn's face floated easily into his mind. As he tuned Eiona's voice out, he returned in his mind to happier times.

And this time, his memories stayed true.

* * * * *

Eiona drew back her foot to kick the sleeping idiot's side but Eilrah said quietly, "He did save your life, little one."

"And that one good deed wipes out the wrongs he has done?" she demanded, turning to glare at Eilrah, feeling betrayed. He was hers, this dragon. She had trained for years to learn to be worthy of him, of her gifts. She had been trying to summon him for months, searching for the strength, searching for the magic.

And when he was finally here, he defended the man she hated.

"He is not the man you knew before," Eilrah repeated. "And the priestess inside of you will see that."

"I see nothing," she snarled.

Lifting his head, he glared down at her from his still rather impressive height, a good sword length over her head even in his smaller form. "You will. It is your duty to seek the good in all you meet. So *seek* it, *priestess*." And then he turned on his hindquarters and slid off into the night.

Duty?

My duty?

That...that...overgrown lizard had the nerve to tell her about duty?

Eiona flung herself down on her makeshift pallet, and immediately wished she hadn't. Her body had taken too many abuses recently, and not enough food and rest. Every bone and muscle cried out sharply at her treatment and she wished she had shown a little more care.

She lay still, not using real magic, but soaking up the energy of the land beneath her, from the air around her, until it soothed her battered body and nerves. Too bad the land couldn't do the same for her state of mind.

Eilrah. Her long awaited *Orinduuc,* finally, finally, had come to her. And he dared to tell her that she wasn't doing her duty.

Criticize her. Over Rue.

Rue Abulein, one of the biggest bastards she had ever met. An evil, cruel, coldhearted, soulless snake of a man.

Who just so happened to be lying on cold earth, one arm flung over his eyes, a solitary blanket between his body and the floor of the cave. While Eiona slept on piled furs, and leathers, and, unless she was mistaken, some of his clothing. Just beyond his reach, curled up in her little nest.

"Damnation," she muttered under her breath. Rolling on to her side, she snagged one of the looser cloths and tugged it over her body.

She deserved the extra blankets, damn it.

She was hurt, half starved, and recovering from a terrible ordeal.

But Rue would never have thought of that. Would never have used his blankets and bedroll and clothing to make her more comfortable.

"Damnation," she repeated before closing her eyes and willing herself to sleep.

Chapter Four

ഔ

When she awoke, it was to feel divine heat, all along her front half. To feel a large warm palm cupping her bottom, while she curled against a broad male chest, a steady slow heartbeat just beneath her ear.

She froze.

Rue.

He sighed in his sleep, shifted, and moved, until he was cuddling her on his chest, his face nuzzling her neck.

That large palm started to stroke her ass through the shirt that was slowly and inevitably riding up, while his cock pressed against her belly. She started to cuddle against it, instinctively, until she remembered.

With a hiss, she jerked straight up, locked her arms, and shoved against him. "Let me go, you ass," she snapped, jerking free of him.

His eyes opened slowly, reluctantly. Yawning, he reached up and scrubbed his hand across his face before he sat up, staring at her with a grim face. "Nice wake up call," he muttered.

A wake up call? What on earth is a wake up call?

Scowling at him, she coolly said, "I'd appreciate you keeping your hands away from me."

"You came over to my side, darlin', not the other way around," he replied, shrugging his shoulders and shoving to his feet. True enough, the little nest of blankets were a good arm's reach away, and she had left the softness of her nest, for the warmth and security of a warm male body.

A massive erection strained the front of his breeches, but he paid it little mind. And her even less, as he walked out of the cave to study the watery, early morning light.

She bit back the reply that lingered on her tongue as she slowly got to her feet. And tried to convince herself she wasn't sulking because he hadn't tried to pursue it, at least a little. He had every right to think it *was* his right.

After all, they were bound to each other. And most *elai* did wed their priestess and—

"Hell and damnation," she swore hotly. "What in the hell is wrong with me?"

Kye idly wondered the same thing as she moved around inside the cave while he knelt at the side of a creek and splashed icy water on his face.

"What am I doing here?" he muttered wearily. For what seemed like the thousandth time.

"Haven't we already discussed this?"

Turning his head, he watched as Eilrah settled his massive body down beside the creek. Even in this more condensed form, he was enormous, breathtaking, and disconcerting. "I don't know what I am supposed to do," he said bluntly. "Where am I supposed to take her?"

"I was trying to make it easier on you," Eilrah said, sounding rather weary himself.

"By taking what little I have left of myself away?" Kye asked tiredly, shaking his head.

"If you wouldn't insist on fighting it—"

"Not fighting it? You are trying to change what is, what was. Trying to change me," he argued, jabbing a thumb at his chest. "I'm thinking thoughts that aren't mine, feeling feelings that aren't mine, behaving in ways that don't feel right. How can I not fight that?"

"You need his knowledge of this world," Eilrah said stubbornly. "You said it yourself. You don't know what to do. He would know."

"I am *not* him. Don't try to make me him," Kye argued. "Fuck." He got to his feet and stomped away, hardly noticing that even as he moved away in temper, he was silent. Eerily so.

Hardly noticing that he grabbed his bow as he left the tiny camp. And didn't he even realize how natural, how easy it was for him to use that bow to take down an odd little creature that looked like a miniature deer—only solid, stone gray, with eyes the color of emeralds.

It wasn't until he was half way back to the camp that he wondered at this knowledge he had. But he still had *himself*, his own personality. And his memories.

"Why aren't you crowding my mind, lizard?" he asked softly, stopping in his tracks.

When only silence answered, he laughed. "Oh, come on. I know you're there. Why aren't you pushing his thoughts into my head?"

A loud sigh seemed to echo through the forest and collect in front of Kye. Reaching up, he rubbed at his eyes with one weary hand while Eilrah coalesced in front of him. "Do you have to do that?" he asked once Eilrah had taken solid form.

"I will give you one honest answer to one honest question," Eilrah said, smiling with his eyes, with the way his great mouth gaped open. "Is that the one you want me to answer?"

"You've made it clear you plan on forcing his thoughts on me. Am I going to be able to be *me* or will you turn me into him?"

Eilrah huffed out a steamy puff of air. "*You* have already made it clear that forcing it on you won't work. I've tried and you keep shoving me out. You've an astonishing amount of will power, do you know that? And I wasn't trying to force him on you. I was merely allowing the barriers between your personality and his knowledge to . . .waver. Eventually, what *he* knew you will know."

"And that is possible how?" Kye snapped, dropping the carcass to the forest floor and stubbornly planting his feet, folding his arms across his chest.

"You are the how. Damnation, your head is like a rock. I can't change you if you so clearly don't want changing." Dropping to the ground and eyeing the carcass with rather clear greed, he continued, "But Rue is gone. At least, the man who called himself Rue. That is *your* name now."

"So deal with it, right?" Kye asked with a laugh.

"Mmmm. Since he is gone, there is no reason I cannot allow you to have what he knew. And since you so adamantly insist on keeping your memories intact, since you insist on being *yourself,* then so be it. But it is most un-warrior like." And then the dragon was gone. Again.

Into thin air.

"Insanity starts looking more attractive by the minute," Kye muttered under his breath.

"Rue. You're Rue," he whispered to himself under his breath.

And then he sighed.

"No. My name is Kye."

* * * * *

Eiona couldn't stop watching him.

He wasn't acting like himself.

And that was reason enough to distrust him. He had come back into camp, whistling under his breath. He had wished her a good morn, of all things. And he had pretended not to notice when she had bathed earlier. She was actually quite certain that he had avoided looking in her direction.

And Eilrah, her *Orinduuc,* acted disappointed with her when she had seethed under her breath about the bastard not fooling anybody.

And of course, she hadn't looked. There was no reason for her to search his soul. She had already done it once and he had been a cesspool—the contact with his soul had left her feeling dirty for weeks. She wouldn't do it again.

He had awkwardly cared for the myriad scrapes she had sustained, and Eiona was certain that Eilrah had been guiding him along silently. Which bothered her even more. He shouldn't have that silent communication with her creature.

Of course, Eilrah acted as though he weren't her servant.

I am not your servant, *little sister,* a voice blasted into her mind, making her stumble. It seethed with indignation and pride.

And it came from Eilrah.

Resting against the tree she had landed against when she stumbled, she slowly turned her head and stared at the seething creature behind her. She hadn't noticed before, but when he was angry, his golden scales tended to glitter red. Glittering now so brightly that he near shone with it.

She wasn't even aware Rue had turned to glance at her, then stop.

"You are mine," she contradicted. "I called you, and you came to me."

"I am not a genie, nor a demon you can conjure. I am your companion, your friend, if you let it happen. But *not your servant,*" he hissed, his neck arching and his black tipped tongue lashing out. "I am a Grand Dragon of the Ninth Order, with Golden rank, child of a Rubied Priestess and her mate, and you dare to call me a servant?"

"I summoned you," she said. "I was finally able to master the call and the magic, and I called you. We are bound."

As he spoke each word out loud they echoed in her mind, down her spine, rattling her further. "Exactly. We are bound.

We, not I. Not you. *We.* If I am your servant, then you are every bit as much mine. Perhaps-"

"Eilrah. Enough."

His red eyes flashed to the man who had come up behind her. "Stay out of this," he warned. "She is an arrogant, spoiled child who has been coddled far too much."

"Coddled?" Rue sputtered, his eyes wide. "She was kidnapped, molested, abused, and starved. That's being coddled?"

"No. But if it weren't for those...circumstances, *you* wouldn't be here. But before that? Yes, the child has been coddled. Her every wish, her entire life, has been catered to. She wanted a pretty piece of jewelry? She received it. She wanted a gold eel for breakfast? Five hunters went after it. A new lodge? Others all but stripped their homes bare in order to make her new home the finest. Yes, she is a spoiled child."

"And she thinks I'm going to be yet another servant in her ever growing throng?" the dragon scoffed.

"She's a kid," Rue said, shrugging his wide shoulders. "And—she's female. From what I've been able to tell, the men here *enjoy* catering to the women."

The men here? Eiona thought, confused, as Eilrah advanced on Rue, his long tongue snaking out, tasting the air around Rue, his large red eyes narrow with fury.

"I am no one's servant, least of all *hers,*" Eilrah spat.

"It sounds to me like somebody has been telling her the wrong shit. That isn't her fault. But this isn't exactly the time to worry about it. Look at her for crying out loud," Rue insisted, throwing a hand in her direction.

He was *defending* her? Humiliation stained her cheeks red. The day she needed a pompous, evil, lecherous ass like him to defend her was the day she breathed her last. "This is none of your concern, Abulein," she said, her voice trembling until she steadied it with sheer will.

Eilrah's eyes came back to hers, his eyes burning. In a scathing tone, he said, "Eiona—"

And Rue stepped between them, reaching up, warding the dragon off. "Enough, dragon. Enough. She isn't well and she's been through hell. Don't you think the etiquette lesson, or whatever the hell you call it, can wait until she is better? Hell, you blasting her with that voice is bad enough. But you're touching her mind as well, I can feel it."

"Human," the dragon growled in warning.

He was going to get himself killed, Eiona thought weakly, forcing herself upright.

"Look at her," Rue said, turning and gesturing to her. "Look."

The fire seemed to dim, and then fade, from Eilrah's eyes as his gaze met hers. His neck lost the tension and he seemed smaller, less dangerous.

"Can't this wait?" Rue asked again, softly. "She's been through enough. Hell, she's just a kid."

Her head flew up and she glared at him indignantly. "I am not a child," she hissed, shoving away from the tree.

Only to stumble, and fall, right up against him, her bare hands coming in contact with his bared arms as he caught her, swearing under his breath.

Too much contact. She yelped, wanting to jerk her hands away from his naked skin before the contact started.

But it was too late.

Instead of the disgusting pictures she had last glimpsed, she saw something else.

Someone else. And for a few brief moments, she became that someone else.

Images blasted her, memories and emotions firing from his soul into hers. Her fingers contracted on his flesh as a large metal creature came rushing at him, pain streaking through his body, bones snapping, his body flying.

A woman with wavy, red hair was staring down at him, her eyes heartbroken and full of tears, as she stroked his face.

Standing in the middle of a place that seemed filled with magic, rolling green hills and ancient circles of stone, ruined castles and towering cliffs above a majestic beach.

Lying on a bed, with tiny little strings connecting his broken body to boxes that beeped and whined and whirred and fed fluid into him through a tiny hole in the flesh of his arm. The woman again, tears flowing freely down her cheeks as she whispered, "I love you," over and over.

The same woman pressed between two hard male bodies, moaning and crying out with pleasure under their hands, their mouths, as Eiona watched from the mirror, feeling the tight silk of the woman's body embracing her flesh. Only she didn't have the flesh that was being embraced.

Cold water splashed her face and when she looked into the mirror, it wasn't her face she saw. It was a man's, with dark brown eyes, silken black hair the color of a raven's wing, sharp cheekbones. Rue's eyes. In the wrong face. She realized she was trapped inside that body —seeing and feeling his memories.

Another field, full of stones and statues, with that woman being held by another man.

Finally, she was able to wrench her fingers away and she fell back onto her rump to stare up at him.

And she saw what Eilrah had already told her to look for. Another man, trapped inside Rue's body. It was there, in his eyes, warm gentle eyes so out of place in that warrior's face. The body of a protector. The soul of a warrior.

The heart of a lover.

"By the ninth order, who are you?" she asked shakily.

He had felt it—felt his memories, his life as it burned a path from his soul into hers. And Kye started to understand just a little of what Eiona was, what being a priestess meant. And he knew what she had seen.

It had all come back.

The accident, the pain of suffering inside that broken body for hours that had stretched on and on without end, while he held on, while he waited for Ashlyn— to see her one last time. The months he had suffered as he watched Ash, the soul-eating jealousy of seeing her with another man, even his best friend.

He went to his knees, pressing his fingers to his eyes.

He wasn't ever going to see Ashlyn again.

He was well and truly gone from her life, and their world.

Stuck in this one, to be known by everybody as a bastard, a son of a bitch who abused women, molested young girls, and used drugs to seem more a man.

"Go away," he rasped when a gentle hand touched his shoulder, safely covered by his jerkin. A jerkin, for crying out loud. No more jeans, no more Sunday football, no more long Saturday night drives followed by slow gentle sex on the hood of his car.

He'd never go back to Ireland—where his parents had met and fallen in love, where he had been born and spent so many summers. Never go fishing with Connor at the lakes in County Kerry, never walk along the Cliffs of Moher again and stare into the crashing waters.

No more Ashlyn.

He was stuck here, away from her, lost to her. He would never bury his face in her hair again after hitting the snooze button, stealing five more minutes with her under the covers. And he'd never mount her soft, sweet smelling body and ride her until they both collapsed from the pleasure.

"Rue."

He heard her say his name several times, but it took a few moments before he could get the stiff muscles of his neck working so that he could stare at her. Woodenly, he said, "Kye." And then he tore his gaze away from that exotic face with the worried eyes.

"Kye," he corrected softly. "My name is Kye, and I want to be alone right now." He sat there, listening as they left, while he mourned his life.

Chapter Five

✂

"Why didn't you warn me?" she whispered, glancing behind her to the familiar body that held an unfamiliar man. The lifelessness in his eyes just now tore at her, the pain and the loss.

A good man.

She had felt it—the purity, the goodness of his soul. The true soul of a warrior, a worthy *elai*. One she had shunned and insulted. He didn't even know who he was, or why he was here, and he had saved her.

"Nine hells, I *am* a child," she muttered.

They stopped by the creek to wait. He would find them, she knew.

Then she turned and met the dragon's eyes squarely. If she had wronged her *Orinduuc* as much as she had wronged the stranger who had called himself Kye, then she'd best face up to it.

But first.

"Why didn't you warn me?"

The dragon, shifted and seemed to shrug. "I thought I had."

"You made it seem like Rue had merely changed. That is not Rue," she said slowly, embarrassment starting to flush her face red. "That is another man stuck inside Rue's body. A good man. And he doesn't even know why in the hell he is here. I felt his confusion, and I felt your touch on his mind. Why did he save me? And why were you trying to touch his mind?"

"You truly are young," Eilrah muttered, shaking his great, spined head before sighing. "He wasn't supposed to remember. I tried to take the memories, to make this easier on him. He fought. And if he fights, forcing it on him could destroy the fabric of who he is.

"*You* weren't supposed to know. In time, you would have come to know who he is now, not who you thought he was. Things would have been as they were meant."

"He had a lady," she said stiffly. "A woman who loved him, and he loves her still. How can he be true to me, loving another woman? He adored her, damn it. She is his entire world."

There was little else that would draw a priestess. Oh, a lovely body was indeed a benefit. But some of the priestesses she had known had been bound to an *elai* who was plain, or sometimes truly homely. But there had been love, and need, and pleasure, and lust. Because those men had been great in soul. Worthy of loving, worthy of giving love. Able to protect, but willing to be protected as well.

Their souls had all shone, with a soft golden light.

The man she had just touched had a golden light.

He had given his heart away, to a woman with a winsome smile and laughing eyes. She had felt it, the surety, the rightness, of that love. And knew what she had felt for Aiken had paled.

This was a man she could love. One she would have happily bound herself too. The kind of man she had hoped, prayed her *elai* would be.

A strong man who would love her. That she would love in return. A sure, certain love. And he belonged to another.

"She is lost to him."

"Because you took him," she said, her throat tight, her voice bitter. Had that beautiful, dark skinned, dark eyed man been pulled from his world because of her?

"No. I did not take him," Eilrah said softly. He slumped and rested his head on his foreclaws. "He was hurt, gravely hurt, and his body was dying. I found out just in time to bring him here. You see, he was supposed to have been born here, for you. You were meant for each other. And I was made aware by the Divine what had happened. I took a chance, and brought him here. His body was dying, Eiona. He isn't here because I took him from *her*. I took him from death."

The bands on her chest loosened a little. At least she wouldn't have that weight to bear. It wasn't her fault that sure, certain love had been torn apart.

Slowly, she sunk to the ground, feeling unbelievably bitter. For a moment, it had seemed that beautiful pale body could have been hers, that she could fall asleep against him and wake wrapped in his arms, tangled in that dark gleaming red hair every day. That strong, proud heart she had seen the instant she had touched his bare flesh could have been hers.

"But his heart belongs to her," she whispered.

The woman whose name was Ashlyn.

Not Eiona.

* * * * *

His eyes itched and ached.

They had been moving since he had risen from the ground roughly mid-morning. It was now probably close to midnight; of course, without a watch, how was he to tell?

Eiona rode atop a horse he had gotten from a village. The villagers had all but lifted her up and bodily placed her on it, so eager were they to help a priestess. They had tried to push him onto one, but he had refused. It didn't seem right. He hadn't earned the adoration and awe and respect he saw coming from them.

If they knew anything about what the man called Abulein had been, they would have been disgusted.

Kye knew. The longer he was inside this body, the more those vices made themselves known.

And it was getting hard to tell which vices were Rue's, and which were his.

One thing was certain. They both had a real hard-on for the lady Eiona.

He walked along side the horse, making certain she could ride in her weakened state. Even though she argued, without meeting his eyes, that she was fine.

And while he walked, he grew aware of just how finely tuned Rue Abulein's—the warrior's—senses had been. He could hear birds as they flew above him, hear the creek and smell the water, even though it was nearly a mile away. And Eiona was close.

So close. Her smooth supple honey gold skin smelled of musk, vanilla, and sweet, sweet woman. Her glossy black cap of hair lay close to a finely molded skull, making her look vaguely pixie-like. Large almond shaped eyes that wouldn't meet his only adding to the illusion of myth and magic.

Hell, there was no myth.

Only magic.

Her unfettered breasts pushed against the rough cotton of the shirt he had given her, her dusky nipples erect almost every time he glimpsed them. Damn it, he thought silently. He couldn't keep his mind off her, of how she smelled. Wondering how she would taste and feel.

Or how she had looked, as he had watched from behind that barrier while she fucked her lover.

And now she slept astride her horse, her body rocking in rhythm, while she rested over the horse's broad shoulders and neck.

Kye kept walking, one foot in front of the other.

He ached.

His entire body ached.

And he figured, if he walked long enough, he could collapse and sleep without dreams, without knowing where or what he suddenly was.

And maybe he could forget the fucking pity he had seen in her eyes. Or how tempting it would be to play on that pity.

It had been *months* since he had buried his cock inside a warm, wet pussy— since he had savored the taste of a woman's cream as she climaxed under his mouth.

Save for the one ghostly night he had been allowed to join Ashlyn. That had been bittersweet, and too damn short.

It would be a cakewalk to use that pity to get closer, to take what he was certain she'd offer.

And then he would be the most pathetic of all creatures.

A pity fuck.

He laughed sourly, stumbling over a large root that covered nearly half the path. Not while he was still in his right mind.

"You need to rest," a rough voice said from behind.

"I'm fine," he said curtly. He had little to say to that damned overgrown lizard. If Eilrah hadn't been having a pissing contest with Miss Arrogance, Kye wouldn't have ended up touching her, bare skin to bare skin, and maybe these memories that coursed through his mind like electrical volts wouldn't have started. These weren't the slightly hazy, sweet memories he had been having.

These were vivid, almost painful, almost hallucinations.

Maybe…if he hadn't touched her.

And maybe he wouldn't have started wanting another touch of her flesh.

"Warrior's body you may have, enhanced senses and stamina, you may have. But your heart, your mind, and your soul are weary. Take your rest," Eilrah insisted.

"Go. To. Hell."

And he kept walking.

Behind him, Eilrah snarled under his breath, "Mortals. Hopeless, the whole fucking lot of them."

Then Eilrah hissed in outright disgust as he realized what he had said. "Damnation, it is contagious! Now I'm talking like him."

It was beyond midnight before he gave up and made camp. A very shabby camp—but he was too tired to do more than rig a rough shelter, with more stolen knowledge, for the priestess.

He curled a long leather cape the villagers had insisted he take around his shoulders—sprawling his unfamiliar long body on the ground, yearning for a soft air-chambered mattress, satin sheets, and his wife.

He fell asleep drifting and imagining two women.

A red-head with laughing eyes and a loving smile on her face.

A sultry brunette who sulked and pouted and made him burn.

The sultry brunette rose before dawn, but she remained quiet, padding her way through the tangled woods around the camp, reluctant to draw too close for fear of waking him.

She knew how late they had traveled, knew why he pushed himself so hard. To try getting past the memories she had unwittingly stirred up. If Eiona wasn't so embarrassed about what she had done, she could have soothed those memories away. But she couldn't do any soothing while she was in so much turmoil herself.

Touching him had done her nearly as much damage as it had done him.

He wasn't the only one who was reliving those memories in vivid detail. Eiona had felt the touch of his hands as they both relived the memories. Knew the feel of his heart, the depth of emotion that he had felt for Ashlyn, his mate. Knew how lost he felt without her.

She now knew his touch, knew his scent, his taste.

All things she could have done without.

She dropped to her knees beside the clear running stream, her breath fogging slightly in the cool morning air. The fog grew heavier as she started panting, reliving those memories once again. She was inside that woman, the rounded pale shape of her, feeling fire course through her as the dark skinned man she recognized as Kye worked his way down her body.

When Eiona's fingers slid beneath her borrowed trousers, it was Kye's hand she felt. When she slid her fingers over her still bare mound, it was his lips she felt caressing her naked flesh. Pinching her clit felt like his teeth biting down gently. And she felt the wet, gentle caress of his tongue when she started to glide her fingers in and out of her wet passage.

Falling to her back, she continued to caress herself, riding the wave of stolen memories until she came in a wet geyser, her cream drenching her hand and the crotch of her trousers.

"If you're done, we need to get going."

Her eyes flew wide, but she was too drained to move. Rolling her head, she stared at Kye from across the distance that separated them. Drawing her hand from her pants, she held out glistening fingers and said in a low, husky whisper, "Why don't you join me?"

A reddish brow lifted. Her vision blurred, and superimposed over his taller, broader form, she saw who he had been, shorter, dark skinned, his eyes laughing and hot with love and lust. When he moved in her direction the vision fell apart and she saw the man inside of Rue's body as he came to kneel by her side.

When his hot wet mouth closed over her fingers, she gasped. She hadn't expected much reaction at all—much less this. But all he did was lick the cream from her fingers, stroking his way to the center of her palm and pressing a kiss there before he rose, pulling her to her feet.

"You don't mean that," was all he said before he retreated, and disappeared back into the woods.

Staring at his retreating back, she said, "Yes. I do."

But she sighed and stripped off her clothes, wading into the waist high water, ignoring the cold water as she quickly washed.

Chapter Six

ဆာ

The spicy sweet taste of her lingered on his tongue as he finished destroying the small crude shelter and securing their things to the horse. It didn't feel quite as awkward as it had last night. But it didn't feel right.

His cock was still pressed hard and full against the lacings of his trousers. Kye had to admit it felt less uncomfortable than it was when you had a hard on while you were wearing jeans. The leather, soft and tanned, cupped his flesh, stretching with him, instead of binding him tightly the way heavy denim did.

You shouldn't have watched her.

Hell, he knew that.

When he had followed the sound of soft, breathy moans, he knew what he was going to find, but he hadn't been able to turn away. This damned hearing of his was so acute, he had heard her over the crashing of water and the noise of the forest.

All he could see was the movement of her fingers and hand beneath the covering of her clothes, but he could smell her, smell the sharp increase of her scent as she worked herself closer and closer to climax. He had wanted to move to her, and finish the fucking she had started by herself.

But he hadn't.

He had just watched as she masturbated herself to orgasm. And when she had offered her wet fingers, he had sucked the cream from them, fighting the urge to rip her pants off and drive into her.

The soft rustling behind him was the sound of her returning to camp. The sun was just edging over the sky, turning it a lovely shade of deep, deep lavender. He wondered what it was that made the sky so different here. Instead of blue, it was almost always shades of purple. Deep royal purple at twilight and sunrise, edging its way to a soft, pale, pale purple as the yellowish white sun rose higher into the sky.

"If you want to eat, do it. We need to get going," Kye said when the rustling stopped. He could smell her, standing just behind him.

She sighed, her breath warming the back of his shoulder as he continued to strap and adjust the bags on the horse. Or whatever it was. It was definitely horse like, with a broad chest, four long powerful legs like a Clydesdale, but with a longer, serpentine neck, and a wider, spade shaped head. Its ears flopped forward, just slightly, like a Labrador's and it had gentle green eyes— kind and intelligent.

"You should rest," she said softly. "You slept so little last night."

"I'm fine," he responded.

"No. No, you're not. I...I know what I did, and even though it was unintentional, that makes it no easier to bear. Such a touching makes you weary and you have not rested well a single night since you saved me. Longer than that."

"I am fine, priestess," he repeated, aware of more of the taboos of this strange land. Touching her had ensured that. So many things that hadn't been clear now suddenly were. Her name was all but verboten, allowed only those close to her. All others must address her as priestess, wise one, lady.

"Eiona," she said softly, her eyes narrowing on his face. He watched from his peripheral vision as her full mouth flattened and firmed with stubbornness. "Call me by my name, Rue. I mean, Kye."

"I haven't that right," he said just as stubbornly.

She blew a frustrated breath out and shoved a hand through her short locks. "I am sorry, Kye. Truly sorry. I am sorry to have caused you such pain. The memories will not always be so vivid. They will fade, to what they were before we touched," she said. "It may take a few days, but soon they will be less painful, less vivid."

"You need to eat," was all he said. He moved away from the horse, and then stopped. She wasn't going to let it go. He knew it. Cocking his head, he stared back at the animal and asked Eiona, "What kind of animal is this?"

It was odd, what memories, what knowledge he could glean from what remained of Rue. But he didn't know what this creature was. Didn't know exactly where they were going until they were already nearly there.

"It's a rean," she said, her voice sullen and sad. The look on her face made him all too aware that she knew he was tired of talking about anything personal with her.

"A rean."

"A farm animal, mostly. But it doesn't mind riders and can travel long distances with very little food or sleep or water. The villagers who gave him to you were very generous. He is worth a great deal."

"Then why give him to strangers?"

A pause, and then in a tone of surprise she answered, "Why, because we needed him."

Sure, why else?

Kye ran his fingers through his hair, grimacing at the unfamiliar feel and texture. He used a cord and tied it back out of his face as he dropped to sit on an exposed tree root, then tore into the meat strip he had kept from the packs.

Across from him, Eiona did the same, watching him closely.

He pretended not to notice as he ate the salty meat and washed it down with water. The water was odd, sweet and slightly fruit flavored. It had come from the well in the village, and even though they had left it behind several days ago, it remained cold and fresh. It was running low though.

Behind him, Eilrah rumbled, "We shall reach the outskirts of the *Oriniic* within a few more weeks. There is a fresh spring ahead where we can refill our skins. We will be there by nightfall and should have enough water left to last us."

Eiona reached up and ran her fingers through her short cap of hair. It was close to two inches long now, and wispy soft. Kye averted his eyes when she lifted her head—instead glancing over his shoulder at the dragon. "What then?"

"Eiona will rest, regain her strength. And then we hunt the one who did this," Eilrah said softly.

"Not we," Eiona said before Kye could speak. "This doesn't involve you, Kye. You saved my life and I am grateful, but this is my responsibility, not yours."

He paused in the middle of taking a drink, lowered the flask and capped it slowly, while he ran those words through his head. "Great. Just fucking great," Kye said. "And would you mind telling me exactly what is my responsibility? I don't belong here, I never asked to come here, but I am stuck here and the only thing that seems to be an option for me is doing whatever in the hell that dragon brought me here to do."

Eiona said softly, "He was wrong to bring you here. This was a mistake and I am sorry."

A mistake.

Is that all it was to her? No matter how bitter he was over losing Ashlyn and losing his life, he knew if Eilrah hadn't brought him here, he would be well and truly dead.

And to Eiona, this was a mistake.

"That's great. Lovely. Will that get me back home? Get me back my life? My wife?" he demanded, rising slowly to his feet, watching her oblivious face. She didn't understand. "Can you get her here? Bring her to me?" She really couldn't figure it out, why he was so angry.

Confused, she shook her head and said, "No. I cannot do that."

"I see. So I'm not welcome at your side, which according to him," he jerked his head to the silent dragon, "is where I am supposed to be. You can't return me to where I belong. You can't give my wife back. You can't bring her to me. And I don't have a clue what to do in this world. No clue where I belong, how to make a living, unless I follow the memories that are in my head. But you don't want me doing that. Because you are not my responsibility and my being here is a mistake. Shit, I probably can't even find my way back to where the body's home is. Much less have any idea how to survive here.

"Let's not talk about the fact that if that bloody dragon hadn't brought me here, I would be nothing more than a corpse in the ground," Kye added nastily. "After all, my body—the one I was born into—is worm food now."

"But you're sorry. That really makes it easier," he finished, shaking his head and lifting his sword, then sliding it home in a movement that felt so easy, so natural, and so completely alien.

Then he strode off into the woods, following the path he had abandoned only hours earlier.

Eiona stared after him in confusion.

"He has one purpose here, Eiona. All knowledge he has is related to that purpose. And you are trying to rob him of that," Eilrah said from behind her.

"It's not his responsibility," she repeated. "I thought he would be glad to be rid of us. Of me."

"You are all he knows, all he has left," Eilrah said. "What is he to do? While he may have Rue's knowledge, his abilities, he isn't Rue. He's just a babe in the woods right now. And the one thing he can do, you don't want him doing."

"Why should he want to?" she demanded, bewildered.

"I imagine trying to help a woman is part of what he is. But it goes beyond that. He may not want to, but it is all he has right now."

"Men," she mumbled, ignoring Eilrah as she gingerly mounted the patiently waiting rean.

"Yes," Eilrah said to her retreating back. "Men. He is a man. And the one thing he has right now to keep him grounded is a man's responsibility that was forced on him when I brought him here. He's accepted that, and is willing to do it."

"He doesn't owe me this. He owes me nothing," she argued. "He saved me. It is not fair to ask him to fight a fight that isn't his. Is that how I repay him, by forcing him into this?"

"No. He owes you nothing. But you, perhaps, owe him something."

"Fine. He will be paid-"

"Bah," Eilrah spat, stalking closer to her and peering into her eyes, his nose just an arm away from her. "Money? He was taken from everything he knows— died a very painful death and was brought here where he knows nothing save for the knowledge to serve at your side—and you wish to offer him money?

"How much more insulting can you be, priestess? Did the man you soul-touched last night strike you as being that bloody greedy?" The dragon's scales were glittering with fury and his eyes swirled and snapped—burning with disgust.

Eiona slumped, holding the guide rope in limp fingers.

With a hissing snarl the dragon turned tail and stalked off, slithering between the trees, circling around her while he fumed. Long moments later he returned to stare at her and demand, "When are you going to accept that he needs this?

"Without you, he has no purpose. I took him from his life and brought him here to aid you. I thought you would be *happy*, and yet you shun him."

"I never asked for him!" she argued, kicking a leg off of her mount and stomping over to the *Orinduuc*, staring several feet up, into his wrathful eyes.

Eyes that narrowed as he asked in a slithery voice, "Didn't you? From the time you acknowledged what you were, didn't you yearn for a man just like Kye? When you met Rue Abulein, didn't you curse fate and the Divine and demand to know why he wasn't a good man? You asked and prayed for him every time you made offerings to the Divine, every time you made worship, and every time you shared flesh with Aiken.

"You asked," he hissed, his long tongue lashing out from his mouth, flickering around her face, while his breath—hot, and smelling of a wood burning fire—bathed her face. "And I delivered."

Her face flooded with shame and anger as she realized just how right he was. She wanted him. She had yearned for Kye since she was a child, even before she knew what earthly pleasures she would seek with him. Hadn't she dreamed of him—not of someone like him, but *him*— a laughing, dark skinned man with flashing black eyes?

"Take *him*," Eilrah insisted. "His heart, his service. Let him be what he was always meant to be."

"I've no wish to force him into service to me."

"But you take any choice from him by refusing him," Eilrah told her, stalking around her in circles that seemed far too tight for his massive body to make. His spine seemed to curve in impossible places as he wove himself around her like a snake, making it impossible for her to step away, as she had been considering.

"Is that what you owe him?"

She remained silent, remembering the confusion, the hopelessness and the pain she had felt from him the previous night. The dismay and indignation that she had sensed just moments earlier before he had stormed away.

"He needs this."

Eiona slumped, her head falling forward. "I accept," she acquiesced, since the dragon seemed insistent on driving it home. The long, hot serpentine body unwound from her and Eilrah retreated further back and released the restraints on his form, exploding into the larger body that was his true form.

"You accept," he reminded her, his deeper voice vibrating in her chest just before he launched himself into the air, his powerful wings whipping her hair around her face, stirring the trees.

Eiona gathered up the reins and mounted the rean, who had continued to placidly munch forest mushrooms throughout the confrontation. Staring into the sky at the dwindling form of the dragon, she said, "I accept. But you never should have brought him here." And then she urged the rean into a steady pace—following Kye's faint trail—relying on her sense of smell and the rean's to track him as he left her farther and farther behind.

It wasn't her fault.

She sulked well into the morning, and through the brief period they stopped so the rean could rest and feed. She should rejoice, she knew. She had received the man she had yearned for. And part of her knew that if he had come to her heart whole, she would have rejoiced.

Jealousy ate at her like a live thing as she wondered if he could ever truly be joined with her. How could he love her when he so completely loved another woman?

By noon she had thrown off the frustrated mood and exchanged it for a frustration of another sort.

The ground was becoming more familiar, and her body was reveling in it. The blood in her veins responded to it and she felt more alive than she had in months.

It was inevitable, she knew.

Perhaps she should have explained that to Kye.

61

Her connection with her lands was an earthy one. Not a sexual one, exactly. But it reawakened things inside that had lain dormant. Even the itchy, edgy moments by the creek couldn't compare to what was growing inside her as they drew closer to home.

Normally, all this tension would have been without a focus. She had forced herself to focus her attention on Aiken, but the love she had for him had been an easy, friendly one. While sex with him had been pleasing, it hadn't been blinding, hadn't been an urge she could only fight so long.

Now it was focused. And she couldn't fight it.

And she understood why.

No matter how confusing and wrong things might seem, this was how things should have been. Her body had always recognized and been drawn to Rue. It was the woman inside who had been repulsed.

The man now inside Rue's body was anything but repulsive. He drew her.

She could scent him as he moved through the woods—could scent the changes taking place in her body. Part of it was purely timing. Her fertile time was drawing near and a priestess tended to become even more voracious during that time.

Part of it was returning. It was the urge to celebrate her homecoming. Some of it was the slow gradual return of her strength and self. As it returned, as her anger and grief faded away, she could feel the slow, steady surge of life returning. With it, her body reawakened.

But much of it was him—this man who called himself Kye—with his dark, lingering eyes and sad smiles.

Then she saw him.

Licking her lips, she watched as Kye went about setting up camp. He hadn't pushed so late into the night this time, and he hadn't spoken since that morning. Even the brief meal break they had taken at noon, and the quick water and rest break they had taken for the rean, had been spent in silence.

That was all right.

She didn't need him to speak.

Stopping made things a little easier. It would be more comfortable to seduce him while they stopped, as opposed to seducing him against a tree on one of the few water breaks he had allowed them.

She forced herself to eat, smiling slowly when he kept sending quick, assessing glances her way. He could scent the changes on the wind as well as she could—the scent of musk and hungry woman. It was affecting him, even if he wasn't entirely sure what it was he was sensing.

Beneath his form fitting leather breeches, his shaft was hard and full. And the glances he kept sending her way, against his will, became slower and more lingering.

Eiona half expected him to make a move in her direction, but she wasn't really surprised when it didn't happen. This Kye was such a complete stranger, his ways so totally alien. In his world, not all men would take simply because the urge was there, simply because the woman was willing. She understood this, and was surprised to discover she respected that. Respected that he didn't take simply because he wanted. Respected that he governed his body and thoughts and didn't let the desire burning inside him dictate his choices.

But she needed him.

Chapter Seven

ॐ

This isn't going to make things easier between you.

Her head turned slowly, drawn from Kye's long form to meet Eilrah's eyes. The dragon had returned from hunting, his hunger for food sated, and satisfied with the acceptance he had sensed in Eiona.

But worried about what emanated from her now.

I know. But I cannot stop it. I need him.

I know. And I understand. But he may not. At least not yet, not unless you let him.

Let him? she thought warily. *I am not ready for that kind of joining.*

Then I suggest you make yourself ready. Quickly. Otherwise when morning dawns, you will have a whole new set of problems.

She didn't need to let him inside her soul. Just her body.

I understand that it is him *you desire. But he is a stranger here, and many warriors don't fully understand how a priestess can so quickly love a man she just met. Unless you can make him believe how much you want* him, *he will waken feeling like he has been used — a substitute for another man.*

Another man? No other man had done this to her. Not Aiken, not Rue, not anybody.

He should know that. Wouldn't you want to?

He had fallen quickly into sleep, finally giving in to the call of his exhausted body. Eiona had rested lightly, waiting until his body had settled deeply into sleep before she rose.

She stripped down to her skin before she joined him on the single blanket he had tossed down for his bedding. Her body was unbelievably hot. He shifted, one hand curving automatically to cup her bottom as she snuggled against his side, drinking in his scent, his warmth, his life.

Lowering the barriers that separated their souls was easier than she had thought. Holding them erect would have been more of a strain. Especially once she realized how much she yearned to be one with him. She slid one hand down to stroke him through his breeches, letting the merging of their souls guide her to how and what he liked.

Her fingers busily freed him from the lacings and leather before she sat up, staring down at the long, pale perfection of his shaft. It jutted out from a nest of auburn curls, full and hard. Closing her hand around him, she dropped the barriers completely, allowing what he was to join what she was. She could feel his heartbeat as clearly as her own, feel the rush as his blood starting to pound harder through his veins.

Images burned in her brain. She had heard of women and men who enjoyed sex in such a manner, but she had never imagined it. A picture behind her eyes—this man, in his true body, sliding his cock into his lady's back hole while another man shafted her vagina. Eiona wasn't certain how taking his cock into her bottom could pleasure her, but it brought him pleasure. It was one of his needs, which meant she would find a way to fill it.

She knew the minute he awoke. It was right when her fingers caressed the furred sac of his balls. His eyes flew open and he half sat up, staring at her with hot, flashing eyes, his breathing sawing in and out of his lungs. Her nails scraped over the sensitive patch of skin right below his sac just before he caught her wrist and asked, "What are you doing?"

"What we should have already done, if we both were not so stubborn, my *elai*," she purred against his neck as she used a light touch of magic, the element of air, to lift his body from the sleeping mat, allowing her to slip her fingers inside his breeches and slide them down.

"Your soul calls to me," she whispered as she let his body return to the ground, smiling at his wide-eyed look. "Mine calls to yours, do you not feel it?"

"Our souls call to each other, huh? Interesting line you have there," he muttered raggedly. "Is that why you constantly pick fights with me, and try to convince me I have no purpose here?"

She smiled as she slithered down his body. "I was wrong in that. And I like to fight; I cannot help it," she murmured, licking a damp trail up the salty skin of his cock, feeling his hand bury in her short ebony hair.

"Damn it, Eiona. I'm not going to fuck you tonight and be sent away when we reach your home," he snarled, wrenching away before grabbing her, pinning her and rolling atop her. "If you've a need to fuck somebody, fine. You can find a man in the next village. But I won't be used, and I won't be shoved aside simply because I am not useful to you."

Eilrah had been right, she thought. And with a single blink of her eyes, she banished the fragile skins that separated their souls.

A complete merging.

She felt and heard Kye's cry as they sank into each other, as he grew aware of the pounding, pulsing need that lived under Eiona's skin—a need for him. She knew he was aware of the dreams she had lived at night, of the yearning she had hidden from all for so long. How much she ached for him—not for his body—but for all of him.

She felt all his confusion, his rage, his anger, for the time he had spent trapped between worlds, watching helplessly while Eiona herself was taken from her homeland. The fury he had burned with while she was abused and beaten. And his own hunger, a hunger for her.

Not love. Not yet. But he was drawn.

She laughed as his reluctance faded, replaced by the wonder of shucking his mortal skin. *A priestess can go to the spirit lands whenever she wishes, without drugs or meditation, and I can take you with me,* she whispered.

Pain couldn't exist here, in this place of whirling lights and colors. Neither could confusion.

As those emotions faded, they were replaced by hunger and need.

When Kye landed back inside the new body he had been given, he was only aware of the woman beneath him, the scent of her, the powerful heady rush it had given him to know that she desired him, wanted to fuck *him*—not just a man—but him.

Catching her wrists, he pinned them beside her head, understanding also how very hungry her body was. It now made sense—the tense edgy feeling that had filled the air all day. He understood the musky, sweet changes in her body's scent.

"Awfully sure of yourself, weren't you?" he asked, feeling her naked body against his—the push of her lush, full breasts against his chest, the lean, long lines of her torso, the bare lips that shielded her sex.

She laughed and lifted her hips in entreaty, feeling him brush against her. "Not so fast," he murmured. Pressing her palms to the ground, he whispered, "Keep them there." And then he lowered his head, catching one plump nipple between his teeth and pulling, nipping and biting before sucking it into his hot mouth.

Her hands closed into fists as he kissed a path down her body, around her navel before parting her smooth lips and catching her clit in his mouth. The lack of hair made her feel more exposed, more sensitive, and he sensed that. "I am sorry for how they did this, and for whatever reasons." He petted the smooth lips of her labia, and licked a hot path between before he murmured, "But I burn looking at you like this, naked and soft." Lovingly, he bit and nipped at her bare mound before returning to suckle on her clit, groaning in pleasure as her cream started to flow more heavily.

"You are sweet," he murmured, spearing his tongue through her folds. She screamed loudly when he laved her with his tongue, moving her closer to fulfillment. She was so hot and so ready, she knew it wouldn't take much.

When his fingers entered her, she exploded against his mouth, cream ejaculating from her body to coat his lips and face as he pulled back to take in a breath before diving for her again.

She felt the vibration of his words before she heard them. "So damn sweet," he muttered, lapping at the cream that trickled from her pussy. He caught it on his tongue, lapping it up before he started to move upward. "Don't want to go so fast," he said in apology. "But I can't wait."

Eiona stared at him while he braced his body above hers. Lifting her head, she stared at him and urged, "Wait just a little." She squirmed out from under him, staring at his shaft with hungry eyes. His cock was long and thick, with a flared, broad head that bobbed and jerked under her gaze. She caught it in her hand and urged him to his back, sprawling next to him and taking the plump head of his shaft in her mouth. Taking him as far down as she could, Eiona wrapped one hand around his cock, marking her limit, before she started a quick, light suction that had his hips rising to meet her downward strokes.

He tried to pull away as his climax approached but Eiona held fast, purring against his cock, stroking his balls in encouragement, forcing his length down her throat until she nearly gagged. He shuddered and bucked with pleasure, and Eiona did it again, slowly, letting her throat relax around him until she had taken three more inches down.

Lungs burning, she moved in a tiny, maddening rhythm that their merging told her he would like. And like it, he did. His hands buried in her short cap of hair and he held her fast, shuttling his cock down her throat and exploding— while she swallowed his seed and sucked a little more from him before pulling back, gasping for air.

He stared up at her with dazed, cloudy eyes and she smiled as she settled astride his lap, stroking his cock and balls until the semi-hard shaft was like iron again. But when she went to straddle him, he muttered, "No," and flipped her onto her back, covering her body with his, and opening her thighs.

Her tight, wet little sheath clasped him snugly, and Kye sucked in much needed air as he sank half his cock into her. She bucked and writhed beneath him, her head thrashing wildly on the ground. Lowering his head, he caught her mouth with his, parting her lips and tasting her hungrily.

Pulling back, he whispered in her ear, "Can you take us back there again?"

"Hmm," she murmured, thrusting them both into the spirit-land, all of them this time—not just souls, but bodies—so that they lay in the middle of a maelstrom of light, their bodies floating on the rainbows.

He sank further into her as her body relaxed, another quarter of his ten inches sliding inside her; feeling the hot wet hold of her body, feeling her legs come around his hips and urge him further inside. With a moan, he gave her the rest of his length, sinking down until her strong, lithe body pillowed his and he started to pump slowly inside her wet, receptive channel.

Eiona whimpered and rolled her hips against his, brushing her swollen, engorged clit against him—crying out at the contact, begging for more. Kye rolled his weight to one side and reached down, catching her clit between his thumb and forefinger, pinching it lightly before starting to stroke in slow, maddening circles.

All around them, lights and colors danced and flared, growing brighter and brighter as he grew hotter. Her silken walls tightened around him and she laughed at the look of total bliss on his face. She did it again and gasped when he reared back and started pounding her pussy roughly, hungrily, desperately. Dimly, she recalled that he had gone without the touch of a woman for endless months and teasing the tiger wasn't particularly wise.

But pleasant—that it was. He drove his length inside her body mercilessly, teasing and pinching her clit until she was straining against him and screaming for release. She spasmed around him and bore down, tightening around him like glory and he exploded—flooding her body in pulsing wet jets of come—while she shuddered and clamped down on his invading cock in hungry, rhythmic spasms that milked him dry.

They slid from the spirit land into this one like a feather drifting down to the earth, his head pillowed on her chest, their breath coming in ragged pants that slowed and calmed.

Kye could hear the pounding of her heart, feel it as it slammed against his cheek while he gasped for air. Something about her was different—and inside him as well.

He didn't know where the words came from, but he found himself lifting onto his elbows, staring down at her flushed face, saying in a rough, ragged voice, "Born I was to serve at the side of a priestess. I have found the one I seek. Shall I serve at your side forever?"

Eiona's mouth curved up in a smile and she whispered against his mouth, as she pulled him closer to her, "Think now I could go without you, my *elai*?"

* * * * *

Kye knew something inside him had shifted.

But it wasn't because of any dragon's urging or mental meddling. And his memories—those pulsing, painful memories that had tormented him had faded—the painful death of his old body, the gut wrenching jealousy and loss that had eaten at him as Ashlyn slowly fell in love with Connor. Those memories had retreated back to a comfortable haze, where he was certain they would stay.

70

He led the rean the next morning, his body relaxed and easy for the first time since he had landed in this insane world. His heart no longer felt like a raw, painful bruise and he looked around with new eyes.

It was a beautiful world, wild and exotic and untouched by the pollution and neglect of others.

He had the knowledge, buried deep inside his mind, to function in this world. The knowledge seemed to come easier when he wasn't tense, which Kye figured at this point, wasn't going to be an issue. At least not for a while.

He had woken buried inside Eiona's body, his hands already gripping her tight little ass while he bucked underneath her. Her hands had kneaded his chest like a cat and she purred, low and sexy, as she rode him closer to climax.

This woman-child was bewitching.

He absently caressed her calf as they continued down the easy path that was slowly becoming a road, the road that would lead them back to Eiona's home village. They had crossed into the *Oriniic* early that morning, and Kye, through some strange bond with Eiona, had felt the flood of energy that had suffused her, the way the land seemed to open its arms and welcome back its priestess.

Oriniic was homeland, focus and strength to a priestess. Her heart and soul were tied to this land and she would have withered and died slowly if she had been kept from it much longer.

His priestess, *his,* was magic. She could heal the land when it was sick. She could heal the people in time of plague, beseech the Devine for water in times of drought. She could use the elements, like she had last night, using the element of air to move and shift things.

She could call water from where it ran in underground streams and rivers. She could call earth to aid her—asking the trees to hide and conceal or open and lead—and she could call fire.

His priestess was magic.

"How long until we reach your village, Eiona?" he asked quietly.

"Ten days, two weeks, at the most," she answered, her face lifted up to the sunlight that poured through the treetops. "The men who took me traveled for nearly two months, but it was slow going, with them mostly on foot and having to hide their trail."

"Rather odd that they didn't use a mount," Kye murmured with a frown.

"Not so odd. Most animals would balk at trying to carry a priestess where she didn't want to go. The animals know better," Eiona said with a tiny smirk.

Her eyes narrowed and she stared down the path, listening.

Eilrah echoed her movement, cocking his head, and listening then he said, "Men come."

"Men?" Kye asked cautiously. "I hear nothing."

"Neither do I," Eiona murmured. "It is not something I hear, but something I feel."

Kye was unaware that he had drawn his sword until he was staring down the blue-silver length of it, his blood starting to pound in slow heavy beats through his body. Her slim hand landed on his shoulder and she squeezed. "Be at ease, *elai*," she soothed. "They are friends."

It was nearly midday by the time they met up with the friends Eiona had sensed. Two men from her village, one older, one younger. Eiona squealed when she saw them and flung herself from the rean's back and down the path, hurling herself into the younger man's arms with laughter.

Kye stood back, watching with narrowed eyes, feeling the hot burn of jealousy in his gut as Eiona wrapped her arms and legs around the stranger. The older man watched with blank eyes, hiding his smirk behind a cough, and watching as Kye's hands absently caressed the sheathed blade at his side.

Kye ignored him, focusing instead on the man who was just now lowering Eiona to her feet. He was built like a wrestler, maybe six feet tall and almost half as wide through his shoulder as he was tall, with long curly blonde hair and eyes that gleamed as green as emeralds. His hands rested comfortably, familiarly on Eiona's hips. Too fucking familiar with his priestess, and Kye was getting seriously pissed.

A heavy serpentine tail lashed around his waist and Eilrah rasped into his mind, *Easy, my friend. He is friend to Eiona, nothing more.*

Telling me they haven't slept together is a waste. I won't buy it, Kye returned, forcing his hand away from his knife and into a fist.

Such unusual phrases you have, Kye. They have been intimate a time or two, but merely in friendship or companionship. He is no threat—

Kye turned his head and stared at the dragon arrogantly, disdain radiating from him. *Threat? Threat? Do I look threatened? I do not like to see what is mine handled so easily by another.*

You've let your woman be handled by another before, Eilrah reminded him, flashing a picture in their joined minds—of Kye in his old body, Ashlyn sandwiched between his and Connor's bodies, being fucked while she screamed and pleaded for more.

It's not quite the same— consciously deciding to give your lady a double fucking—or seeing another man, that you don't know, grabbing her right in front of you.

Eilrah's lids drooped, a sign Kye was coming to recognize as amusement, and the dragon suggested, *Then why don't you show him your displeasure? He is not your equal and has no right to take such familiarity with her if it bothers you.*

And if she gets pissed?

It is your prerogative to assert yourself, warrior. Start now. Eiona knows protocol as well as I.

Kye turned to see the man still holding Eiona tight, so tightly her tits were squashed against his chest. Her face was gleaming with pleasure and happiness, but Kye saw no sign of true attachment there. With a growl, he crossed the distance between them and asked quietly, "Boy, do you frequently hold your priestess so closely?"

The laughing teen merely shrugged and started to lower his mouth to Eiona's but she turned her head, and her eyes widened as she sensed the anger radiating from Kye. With a veiled smile, she neatly slipped out of the man's embrace and went into Kye's, stroking his mental walls with a soft gesture. As close as she would come to apologizing for making him unhappy. Some women wouldn't have even offered that.

But Kye was learning through this bond, that what made him unhappy made her unhappy, and vice versa. He wrapped his arms possessively around her waist, staring into the narrowed eyes of the younger man calmly, resting his chin on her crown as Eiona asked, "How did you know we were coming?"

"The wise man told us. He had been speaking with someone on the Council and the person had a vision, saying you would come with a new warrior in an old enemy's body," the older man replied, appraising Kye with considering eyes. "I had no idea it would be this one."

"Neither did I," the younger man replied with a sulk on his handsome face.

"Watch your mouth, Eagan," the old man snapped, cuffing the blonde roughly before moving past him and dropping to one knee in front of Kye. "My name is Kar. I know your face, but not your eyes, nor the person I sense inside. I am honored to finally meet the lady's *elai*. Long have we waited."

Kye glanced at Eiona and she offered silently the proper response. He reached out and down, took the man's forearm in his and guided him to his feet. "It is my honor to meet somebody who so truly cares for my lady," he said haltingly, the respectful words sounding awkward to his ears, medieval.

But Eiona beamed with pleasure and the old man's face was wreathed in a glowing smile. "We have come to escort you through the *Oriniic*. We shall hunt and provide and set up your camping sites so that you may spend more time together. A shame to have your bonding moments together spent constantly amove and without true rest."

Eagan merely stared at them with unhappy, jealous eyes.

Sorry 'bout your luck, kid, Kye thought silently.

Later that day, they reached the campsite the two villagers had prepared for them before setting out to meet them. A small shelter—complete with a bed made of springy pine and covered with thick heavy blankets—awaited them and Kye sighed with pleasure as he sank down onto the comfortable nest.

Just as good as a damned featherbed, he decided.

Eiona's weight came down atop him and she curled upon him with a sigh and a smile. "My body aches for a true bed," she murmured.

"What happens when we reach your village?" he asked, stroking up and down her side before resting his hand on the curve of her ass. Eilrah's head poked through the cloth door and he snorted in disgust. "A bed. You have a bed."

Kye groaned and closed his eyes. "Do you mind, dragon?"

The dragon's weight landed on the ground and his head snaked further inside until he could rest his chin beside them on the small nest. "Not at all," he replied with a dragon's laugh.

Eiona grinned at them before curling up by Kye's side, pressed between Eilrah's snout and neck and Kye's body. "We will join in bonding. And then we will hunt the man who stole from the *Oriniic*."

A rumbling voice sounded from behind her. "First she will be ceremonially offered to the Divine, now that her magic has opened. Then the joining. Then the hunt." Eilrah lashed his tongue out and gaped his huge jaws at them. "I must be presented and fawned over, as well. Fresh young sheep, young *weireken*. Sweet wine and sweet lovelies anointing my scales with oils."

Kye cast the dragon a sidelong glance, hoping it could read his mind. "When will we be alone again?"

"Not for a day or two," she replied with a shrug of her shoulders. "The ceremony where I take up the official duty and robes of priestess will take the day and night.

"And we must join at dawn. That will be the day after I am declared priestess, I promise," she murmured.

"So once we reach your village it will be nearly two days?" he clarified.

"Only a little over a day. No need to wait for night. Once we are bound, we can mate by the river…"

"In front of others?" Kye asked with narrowed eyes.

"He comes from a modest world, little sister," Eilrah told her with a laugh. "I doubt he will be so eager to join his flesh with yours in front of an audience."

Eiona's eyes widened and she studied him with pursed lips. "It is tradition that we mate in the open, for all who care to see, the first time after the bonding."

"I don't care for the idea," he growled, his cheeks flushing a dull red as he flashed her a narrowed look.

Her face softened with a smile and she bent low, kissing him gently. "Then we will not do it," she murmured before sliding her tongue into his mouth to taste him. She drew away, a low hum of pleasure on her lips. "We needn't mate in front of others, if my *elai* doesn't wish it."

He slid his hand higher, until he could press his thumb against her wet slit. "I wish it now," he said roughly, pulling her body atop his and jerking at the lacing that held her breeches closed. The knots wouldn't give way and with a snarl he shredded them, watching as her eyes went opaque with excitement.

Casting Eilrah a glance, he lifted a brow.

The dragon retreated with a sigh, grumbling under his breath.

"So do I," she murmured.

He flipped them and moved down on her body, licking her belly, pressing kisses against the flat little hollow, while he palmed one full round breast, plucking the nipple until it was hard and erect.

He felt her moisture coating her cleft and he smeared it around, gathering it on his fingers and using them to paint her nipples with her cream. He sat back on his haunches and lifted her, pulling her legs wide so that she straddled his lap, her folds opening to cuddle his turgid cock. He feasted on her gleaming nipple, while cream dried on the other, drawing the flesh tighter. "Damn it, you're good," he muttered, reaching between her thighs to plunge his fingers into her wet passage.

She keened, rocking her hips against him, guiding his mouth to her other breast, gasping when his teeth closed over the nipple and sucked and licked the cream from it as well.

He started to press one finger against her tight rosette and he was startled when she flooded his hand, coming in a geyser with a scream just at that light touch. She pulled back moments later to stare at him with surprised, wide eyes. "I enjoyed that," she murmured, wriggling against him.

"Never had a cock up there before, have you?" he asked, using her cream to lubricate his fingers and slide one tip just inside, rimming the tight hole, using tiny gentle thrusts to relax her.

"No. But I'll take yours, if it pleases you," she said, her eyes going glassy.

Kye laughed and promised, "It will please you. But we will take it slow."

He moved her away from him and urged her onto her hands and knees, staring at how her position opened her folds, exposing the pink wet flesh to his hot eyes. "Such a pretty little pussy," he purred, bending over and lapping at her. He slid his tongue from her clit and upward, until he could press a kiss to her tight rosette. She jumped and squealed, embarrassed pleasure radiating from her. With his hands on her hips, he held her still and probed at the sweetly puckered little hole with his tongue until she was gasping and moaning and pleading.

Then he straightened and pressed his thumb against her, sliding it inside, and said, "Push against it." She did, and her flesh opened around him, taking the thick intrusion of his thumb in her bottom.

With his other hand, he held his cock steady and started to work it inside her dripping vagina, while she clenched around him, her body already tightened for climax. She was so tight, her tissues so swollen, he had to work it in slowly and he shuddered in bliss as she convulsed around him.

Around his thumb, the walls of her ass gripped him like silk. "It's going to be good, baby, when I sink my cock in there," he said in a low, guttural voice.

"Do it now," she pleaded, reaching back and grasping the cheeks of her ass desperately, trying to pull more of him inside her.

He shook his head slowly as he thrust deeply into her, in slow, gentle movements. "You're not ready yet. It would hurt," he muttered. "We need, ah, damn it, that's good. Need to loosen your muscles a little, otherwise, when I fuck you there, it will hurt you."

"I don't care," she wailed, shuddering around him.

"I do," he replied. No pain. After what he saw while he was trapped, he couldn't bear to see it in her eyes, or feel her recoil from him. He started to work his thumb inside her anus, though, using that erotic stimulus to ease the need growing in her gut.

The flared head of his shaft started to bump against the tiny bundle of nerves buried deep inside her vagina. With a slight change of position, he moved so that each thrust caressed it, and he started to shuttle in and out, staring down at them as his cock pierced her flesh, stretching her, his thumb buried inside her bottom.

She cried out and begged, "Harder."

Kye growled and took them to the ground, filling her with hard furious digs of his cock as she started to shudder and buck with her climax. He felt the wetness inside her pulse and jet around his shaft and he bellowed in ecstasy, his own climax exploding from him in a hot flood.

He pumped repeatedly against her ass, her milking sheath draining him dry, before he curled on his side, pulling her sweet body against him. He smoothed the flat of his hand down her quivering side, smiling as she gasped for air. Nuzzling her soft short hair, he murmured, "I can't believe I won't able to touch your body for two days."

"Touch all you want," she offered, rolling her head back against him. "We are not a modest world."

Cupping her breast in one hand, he tweaked her nipple, making her jump. "I don't do foreplay in public," he said with a grunt as her elbow plowed into his belly. "Sorry."

She rolled around until she was facing him. "Just think how much fun we could have," she purred. "I was thirteen the first time I saw a priestess and her mate…fore-playing in public. They didn't mate, but it was so hot to watch her make him burn."

"Thirteen?" he repeated, lifting a brow at her. "In my world, that is a child. I don't see myself playing with your ass, and kissing your nipples when a kid might see. We will just wait."

She shrugged one shoulder. From under her lids, she asked, "What can I do to loosen the muscles you spoke of? Can it be done quickly?" She stroked her fingers down his naked belly and cupped his shaft, still damp and sticky from her. "I want to feel this in my bottom."

His cock went on red alert, tightening almost painfully. "In a hurry?" he gasped.

"Very much so." Her smiling face sobered and she asked quietly, "Your woman, the one you want to bring here, can you be happy without her?"

His eyes shuttered and he looked away, staring up at the vines that made the roof of the shelter, and the thin swatches of sky visible through it. "There was a time when I would have automatically said no. I loved her, with everything I have in me. I still do, but I also don't think I'm the same guy I was when I had to leave her."

"She is nothing like me, is she?"

"No." Meeting her eyes, seeing the sadness and pain there, he asked, "Why are we talking about this? She isn't mine any more."

A sad, bittersweet smile curved Eiona's mouth and she sat up. Taking her clothes from the twisted pile beneath them, she said sadly, "The question is, are you still hers?"

And then she left the shelter, carrying her clothes in a tiny ball at her waist, her shoulders slumped.

Chapter Eight

&

Why did you ask him? she thought to herself miserably.

Curiosity killed the *keva*, she thought sourly, reminding herself of the tiny rodent like creature with big eyes that would chase a brightly colored ball into a predator's mouth, just to bat that tiny ball again.

Little sister, you must give it time, Eilrah murmured. He came up behind her at the stream where she had bathed in solitude, resting his great jaw on her shoulder, curling his long, wicked tail around her legs in comfort, one wing curving around them, soothing her.

Kye hadn't attempted to find her and the connection between them remained empty. He was hesitant to reach out to her now. Eiona shouldn't have mentioned his woman from before.

What if he changed his mind? What if he no longer wished to join with her?

He cares for you. You have already felt that for yourself.

Cares for me, yes. But can he love me? I am so different from her, and this land is nothing like his.

This is his home now. He has accepted that.

Eiona sulked. *I want more than his acceptance. I want his happiness.*

He will be happy. He can be happy here. Eilrah nuzzled her gently and blew a soft soothing puff of air against her cheek— a dragon's kiss.

There is more. His woman had a way of pleasuring him that I have never done. And he tells me I am not ready for it, she thought, leaning back against the strong body of the dragon. It was

81

easy, so easy to talk to this creature, her *Orinduuc*, this guardian of the homeland. *I want to be able to offer him this pleasure, and I do not wish to be told I am not ready.*

What way is this?

Taking his rod into her bottom. He touched me there, earlier, and the pleasure was indescribable. But his cock is much larger than his thumb and I am certain it will hurt. He tells me there are ways of getting the muscles ready and I want to learn them.

Wanting to pleasure your elai *is a wonderful thing. But do not do it thinking he will leave your body suddenly in love with you. Loving takes time for most mortals. Kye will be no different.*

Eiona rolled her eyes. *I know that, dragon. But I want to be able to pleasure him in the ways he likes. And I want it for myself as well. I want to know every pleasure he shared with her. Besides, it felt wonderful, what he did earlier.*

Eilrah's chest rumbled with a laugh and he nuzzled her with the soft underside of his chin before rising to his feet, towering three feet over her. *I can help with that. I will return. Go to him now. He fears he has hurt you. He is unhappy.*

Unhappy? Eiona ran that thought through her head. He was unhappy. With a slight pout, she thought, so am I.

And then she wished for the dexterity to kick herself.

She hadn't asked to be kidnapped or dragged from her home.

But she had asked for him.

Eilrah was right about that.

Kye, however, had asked for none of this. And she was the one who had put thoughts of his woman in his mind. She had brought her into this.

He was so handsome, so sexy. Just staring at him made her belly clench with need, made her sex go wet with wanting. He towered over her by nearly a foot, and Eiona was a fairly strapping woman, just shy of six feet. His wide spaced, deep brown eyes were nearly black, the pupils almost indiscernible, such dark eyes startling in his pale face. Cascades of dark, deep-red hair fell past his shoulders when he freed it. Right now, it was bound into a tight tail at the nape of his neck.

And his long, pale, battle-scarred body made her mouth water. His wide shoulders tapered down into a lean narrow waist, slim hips, and a tight, muscled butt she was dying to touch again.

She loved staring at him, but it made her eyes blur and water, to stare at him so. Doing so superimposed the man he had been, shorter, a slighter build, with ebony hair and those same dark eyes, full of laughter and love.

Right now, they were dark and blank, his face grim. He ignored the men who sat across from him, staring at him warily, sensing his anger and not wanting to draw attention.

Fools, she thought. *He would harm no innocents.*

Walking behind him, Eiona fell to her knees and slid her arms around his waist and held tight, pressing her face into the valley between his shoulder blades, listening to the pounding of his heart, the air moving in and out of his lungs.

He turned after loosening her grip on his waist, catching her face in his hands and pressing a kiss to her mouth. He drew back just as she was rising and angling her neck for a better taste.

He pulled her tightly against him and without a word to the other two men, took her into the shelter.

* * * * *

Kye rose at dawn the next morning.

Outside, Eagan was already awake and stoking the fire, a small pot simmering over it. He glanced at Kye with veiled jealousy before offering the respectful lowering of his eyes and head before the warrior.

"Don't like me much, do you?"

Eagan stiffened and slowly said, "I have offered disrespect. I am sorry."

Kye shook his head and blew out a breath between his teeth, frustrated. He didn't like the deferential treatment these men exhibited; it reeked of master and serf, and Kye was too much an American at heart to like the things such a relationship implied.

But he was no longer in America.

No longer even in his world.

And he had better get used to it.

There was also an arrogance he hadn't even been aware of that he now carried. Maybe it was remnants from the body's previous owner. Or maybe the arrogance had always been there. Kye had never liked being questioned, had never stayed too long in a place where he wasn't the one in control.

Kye wasn't convinced that he was anybody's better, and probably never would be. Too much land of the free and home of the brave in his blood, too many years of believing in equality, for him to push his beliefs and values aside. But he had a right, a claim, to Eiona, a soul deep bond with her, and this young man, barely out of his teen years, was trying to question that claim.

"Is it me you dislike? Or losing her body?"

"Both. But Kar says you are not the man who came to Aberel years ago, only that you now possess his body. And the dragon respects you. Eion...My lady respects you."

Kye lifted a brow and said, "So it's the losing of her body."

"Being inside her feels like something out of a dream," Eagan said, his cheeks flushing a dull red. His cock was swelling and straining against his breeches and Kye played with an idea.

Nope. Not ready for that.

But some evil streak inside him made him want to pull the kid's strings. Maybe just the rampant dislike he still sensed, no matter what Eagan said. And when he turned and saw Eiona leaving the tent, rubbing her eyes, stretching sore muscles, he gave in. She was naked, unabashedly so, and merely blinked at the two men watching her.

He crossed over to her and took her mouth, deeply, his hands cupping her ass and lifting her against him. He paused long enough to order, "Eagan, fetch the lady what she will need to bathe."

*What are you doing?*she asked silently, her mental touch soft and warm with sleep.

Teaching that kid a lesson. He dropped to his knees and took a stiff nipple in his mouth. He suckled hard, loving it as she went boneless and fell against him with a cry. *If yours is not a modest world, then this isn't a problem, is it?*

She only pressed harder against him and whispered, "I care nothing about who sees."

His cock pulsed against her folds, pressing against the leather that cupped it.

Kye drew away when he heard Eagan return to the camp, with warmed water, rags, and a sullen expression. He flicked a surprised look at Kye when the warrior said, "Bathe my lady."

Eiona slid him a narrow look, but turned to face the other man.

"He wants to be inside you again," Kye said softly, coming up behind her and murmuring into her ear. His cock pressed against her butt while he wrapped one arm around her, cupping the full weight of one breast in his palm, stroking his thumb across the peak of her nipple. "Would it bother you if I let him?"

She arched a brow at him and drawled, "Right now?"

"No. Not now. He hasn't earned it," Kye replied easily, tweaking her nipple and lifting his eyes to stare at Eagan. "Are you going to assist your priestess or not?"

A warmed rag stroked across her brow, her neck. Glanced over her breasts and belly. He slid Kye a wary look and Kye sighed. "Do you really think that is going to do the job? Bathe her, Eagan."

Eiona sighed in pleasure as the man fell to his knees before her and started to stroke the warmed wet cloth over her torso and belly with firm sure strokes, kneading her thighs and calves, massaging first one foot, then the other.

He tossed the rag aside and reached for another, wetting it and stroking her with it between her thighs, glancing up at her face, glancing at the warrior before returning to it.

Kye guided her around, presenting her long slim back to Eagan while he took her mouth deeply. Strong firm hands massaged and stroked her back before stroking the rag down the length of it, past her buttocks down the back of her thighs.

Eagan hands were starting to shake and Kye's heightened senses picked up the scent of his lust, his frustration. And his submission. Which was what Kye had been wanting. The boy wasn't going to continue to stare at Eiona with hot eyes and expect Kye not to retaliate.

Wickedly, Kye decided to see how far he could push it.

Turning her around, he lowered his head to rest his chin on her shoulder, reaching around to cup her breasts while he reached out with his mind to hers. She barely blinked at the contact but flushed when she realized what he wanted.

He is a good lover, she answered silently while Eagan gathered up the rags and tossed them aside, remaining on his knees before them, his hands clenched into tight fists, his cock pressing against his laced trousers, eyes focused in the distance.

Then perhaps...you know I shared a woman before, with another man.

Your woman. Yes, I know.

I'm not ready to share you yet but I want to see his hands on you, his mouth. Are you okay with that?

A slow, heated smile lit her face, turned her eyes hot with lust. *If you mean by 'okay' do I like the idea, I like it very much,* she replied. "Eagan," she said softly. "Fetch us something to lie on."

"Are you going to force me to watch you two fuck?" Eagan asked stiffly, rising to his feet.

"You know I cannot force you to do anything. Neither can Kye, my *elai*. You know he is not the man you met before," Eiona said. "I am not your master. Neither is he. But I am your priestess and I ask this of you."

His shoulders slumped and Eiona glanced at Kye, her eyes full of amusement and reluctant sympathy. *He is young, and full of pride. Do not bruise it unnecessarily, love.*

I don't think letting him touch you will do more than make him hot. And as long as he doesn't try to get between your legs, you can give him whatever release you see fit, Kye assured her.

Eagan returned with a blanket and spread it on the ground. And his eyes widened with shock when Eiona plastered her long, lithe body against his. "He likes to watch," she murmured, throwing Kye a wicked glance as she guided Eagan's hands to her full breasts.

Kye glanced up from unlacing his shirt and shrugged at Eagan's disbelieving look. "I seek her pleasure above all else, Eagan. I want you to know that," Kye said.

Eagan's body spasmed once and his control broke. He seized Eiona and took her mouth greedily, stroking his hands down the length of her body, grasping her ass and lifting her up, guiding her legs around his waist.

Unable to resist himself, Kye took his place behind her, stroking his hands over the exposed folds of her body, dipping his fingers inside the wet well of her sex, drawing out the cream and rubbing it on her tightly puckered anus. His shaft throbbed and pulsed under the confinement of his clothes as he started to rock against her.

Through the bond, he felt her pleasure, felt her lust and enjoyment of being between two bodies, two men so hungry for her. He took her from Eagan who started to curse angrily but fell to his knees quickly as Kye arranged Eiona on the blanket and freed his cock from his breeches.

Eiona cried out when Eagan's tongue speared her wet folds. Kye had shucked his clothes and now crouched over her torso, taking his cock in one hand and thrusting toward her mouth. She opened her lips and took his length eagerly, as far as she could, until her eyes watered and her lungs burned from lack of air.

He marked her limit by circling his hand around his cock and started to fuck her mouth. She was unable to do little more than lie there, buffeted by pleasure as Eagan drank from her dripping passage, and Kye pumped his length in and out of her mouth. Eagan slid two fingers inside, twisting his wrist back and forth with each thrust as he started to nibble on her pulsating clit.

The orgasm ripped through her belly and loins just as Kye jetted his semen down her throat. She jolted in reflex, swallowed, choked a little as he drove his length further down than she had taken it before, until her air supply was briefly cut off. Her lungs ached for air, and a scream built in her gut as Eagan drove his stiffened tongue inside her.

Kye pulled away from her and half fell, gasping for breath as he rolled to his back, lying there staring up at the pale sky. Eiona sucked much needed air into her lungs while the after effects of orgasm rolled through her, leaving her body feeling energized and weak all at the same time.

Eagan caught her eye as she sat up, his hand wrapped loosely around his cock, stroking it almost absently as he stared at her. The moment she met his eyes, his gaze fell away.

She rolled onto her side and slid her hand down Kye's heaving side to his semi erect cock, and she started to stroke, staring at Eagan as she did so. Kye knew what she was planning and he moved as she moved, shifted and twisted until she was kneeling, half propped on Eagan's leg, her butt in the air, opening her folds for Kye.

He probed at her entrance while she caught Eagan's eager flesh in her hand. His eyes were lit with a half mad desire and the moment her tongue came out to taste him, he thrust past her lips, groaning as the walls of her throat closed around him.

He pumped inside her mouth, supporting her upper body with his thighs, guiding her head with his grasp on her hair. As Kye drove his cock inside her vagina, she gasped around Eagan's shaft. He responded by thrusting deeper, until she could take no more. His hips moved in tandem with Kye, one cock leaving her mouth while the other filled her aching sex. Then Kye pulling out and Eagan pumping in, the head of his cock sliding down her throat, leaving her half starved for air.

It was too damn much. The focus of their greed was as overwhelming as it was arousing and her pussy clenched around Kye in climax. Eagan lost control before Kye did and flooded her mouth with salty, bitter seed.

His fingers slid out of her hair and he fell back. Eiona screamed and whimpered as Kye started to fill her with short, hard digs of his shaft, each stroke driving against her womb, bordering on pain. The muscles in her legs felt like water and she could hardly hold her weight up. When he shoved against her again, she collapsed and he followed her down, driving her into the ground while he rode her hard. She felt the press of his mouth, then his teeth against her shoulder as he bit her, marked her. His hips twisted and she screamed hoarsely as it sent her tumbling back down into pleasure, wetness spilling from her as he came deep inside her in hot, pulsating jets.

Then he fell against her, and rolled taking her onto her side, and cuddling her to his chest.

A few feet away, Eagan lay staring at them, his eyes dazed, his body replete.

Eiona said softly, "I'm going to learn how to take you inside my bottom, Kye. I want to feel what it is like to have you both inside me, that way."

Eagan's eyes widened and he paled, glancing at Kye with worried eyes, but Kye only laughed weakly. "Whatever my lady wishes," he murmured against her back.

Chapter Nine

❧

Two mornings later, Eilrah whispered into her mind.

Send the others ahead. Tell them to wait at the river-bend.

She did so, tossing out the order imperiously in her nerves, aware of how arrogant she sounded but too nervous to care.

What did Eilrah have planned?

He had said he could help, and she remembered all too well what she had wanted to hurry along.

Now she was alone and waited in a clearing. She felt the backlash of his wings, felt the wind whip her short hair around her face and looked up. Eilrah landed, one claw drawn up, his body magnificent in his green and gold scales, all edged with ruby-red. The green and gold and violet became less prominent as they marched upwards to his head, until the scales were nothing but red.

And in his hand-claw, something else.

Eiona stared at the long, tapered rod — solid and opaque, ruby red in color — with puzzled eyes before casting Eilrah a curious look. Mindful of Kye and the two villagers just yards ahead, she asked mentally, *What am I to do with this?* It was vaguely cock shaped, and she imagined she knew where it was supposed to go, but it looked odd. Narrow at the tip, widening at the middle, flaring down near the end, and a broad, flat cap on the very bottom.

Her cleft was growing damp with need, with the thought of doing something to prepare her body for the way Kye wanted to take her. She imagined Eilrah was going to tell her how to place it inside, even though Eiona had, finally, figured out what it was for.

She'd seen sex toys before, but Aiken had never cared for them. And Eiona hadn't seen any need.

It was a little embarrassing to think of forcing that tool into her bottom. And more so, for Eilrah to feel the need to explain such. It was bound to be an awkward experience.

My, my, my, how pleasant it was to be wrong.

Moments later, she was on her hands and knees, staring at the ground in utter shock while deep plumes of smoke rolled around her body, caressing, plucking and stroking. One plume had solidified and taken the rod, now slick with some unknown substance and started to rock it against her anal opening.

She flinched at the pinching sensation, biting her lip and whimpering slightly. But another plume had worked its way under her and was suckling on her clit, feeling exactly like a man's mouth.

So much so, she shuddered and bucked with climax when another plume formed into a shaft and started to pump into her dripping passage.

She stiffened, her head falling low as the device in her rear advanced, becoming more and more uncomfortable, stretching her tighter and tighter around the plume-cock that was shuttling inside her pussy.

"Take a deep breath, and push down."

She gasped and lifted her head, staring into Kye's eyes.

He hadn't gone ahead after all.

Instead he was kneeling in front of her, watching with hot, hungry, and faintly disgruntled eyes while hands and tongues of smoke caressed her body as a phantom cock rode her mercilessly.

He glanced at Eilrah, who was curled on the ground, controlling his smoke plumes with absent power, before turning his attention back to Eiona. "Push down, baby," he repeated, drawing her body slightly up, until he had access to her mouth, catching her face and taking her lips roughly, eating at her like a man starved.

She cried out under his touch and her body clenched. When that happened, the muscles in her anus relaxed, and the device slid home, driving seven thick inches completely inside.

It burned and pinched.

But Kye had shifted, and slid beneath her, capturing one hard nipple between his teeth and pulling. His hand slid down until he could play with her clit, rotating and plucking at it until she was crying out and moving hungrily. It caused the device inside her to shift, sending waves of sweet, painful pleasure coursing through her.

A gasp left her when the head of Kye's cock replaced the smoky plumes that had been filling her passage. Opening her eyes, she stared down at him. "Not nice of you to go and play without inviting me," he teased, smacking her bottom lightly in mock chastisement.

"It wasn't supposed to be play," she answered weakly while he worked the thick length of his cock inside. The device had narrowed her vagina drastically, so that Kye had to work his length into her slowly, groaning with pleasure at the tight fit. "I just wanted to be...ah, oh, um...wanted to be able to do this for you."

A hot, sweet smile curved his mouth while he stared up at her. "Let me know if it hurts," he whispered, brushing her hair away from her eyes tenderly. "You're stretched so tight." He started to shuttle his cock in and out while the phantom fingers of smoke continued to play across the naked flesh of her back.

You knew he would come, she hissed in accusation to Eilrah when Kye lowered his head to bite at her arched neck.

Hmm. And now you both can, Eilrah thought, his voice light with mental laughter. *And I can watch.*

Kye's hands went to the plump, rounded cheeks of her ass, spreading them apart, exposing her filled anus to the cool caress of air. "Do you like how that feels?" he asked roughly.

"Yes," she murmured. "Oh, yes." And soon she could take him there.

Maybe even him and another man, her body clenching with pleasure as Kye's fingers dug deeper into her flesh and he rammed his cock upward into her, filling her full, driving her to the fine line between pleasure and pain. Eagan and Kye, both riding her hard…she wouldn't be able to handle it, she knew it.

She creamed against him, moisture flooding from her in wet pulsating waves, as Kye murmured in appreciation and flipped her onto her back, taking her legs and holding them high and wide. She screamed out, feeling the toy inside drive deeper. Kye moved higher on her body, his thrusts rough and hard, as she pleaded for more.

The intense sensations riding inside her nearly drove her insane. She screamed and convulsed around him, but the climax hovered just out of reach. Hungrily, she twisted and bucked under him, seeking more. He reared back, grabbing her legs and draping them over his shoulders, fucking her hard, one, two, three deep, driving thrusts that propelled her into an abyss of pain and pleasure so deep and dark, Eiona wasn't certain she would ever surface.

She sank further into that abyss, while Kye bucked against her and jetted her convulsing sheath full of his seed, holding her in a grip so tight, it hurt.

When she shifted and opened her eyes, long moments later, the slightly painful sensations in her body made themselves known. And became much stronger.

When she shifted and squirmed, Kye's eyes opened and he stared at her with dazed, cloudy eyes. "I need to take this out," she murmured.

Kye's hand slid down over her back and he pressed against it lightly with his fingers. "Is it hurting?"

"No. But my sex aches. It isn't helping."

"If it isn't hurting much, leave it be," he ordered gently, still pressing and stroking the wide base that helped hold it in place. "It will help stretch you. I don't want it to hurt when I take you there."

She shuddered when he lowered his head to kiss her shoulder, a hot, wet open kiss that had her nerve endings sizzling. "How can I possibly want you again?" she whispered. "I hurt and ache from before, and I can still feel your seed inside me, and I'm already hungry for you again."

Kye smiled slightly, stroking her arm with slow gentle caresses. "I'm losing my mind over you," he said quietly. "I move away from you and five seconds later I feel empty. And you expect me to go more than a day without touching you. Then I hear you whimpering and crying out and walk up and find you on your hands and knees while some phantom puts a dildo in your tight little ass."

"A dildo?" she repeated with a frown.

Kye laughed and gently pressed on the toy in her bottom again, a light touch against the flared base before saying, "A dildo. That's what this is called back where I was born. I would've been more than happy to help you put it in, if you had asked.

"Damn it, that was one of the hottest things I'd ever seen, you taking that in your bottom while that smoke caressed you." He nuzzled her nape and said, "You're just so fucking sexy, Eiona. You're driving me crazy."

She laughed weakly and said, "What do you think you're doing to me, Kye?" She rolled onto her back, gingerly, and stared up at his familiar face, at those sweet, gentle eyes that were so unfamiliar. "There were times when I hated myself. After I met Rue, and realized he was so evil, all I wanted was to distance myself from him.

94

"But my body was drawn to him. And he knew it. I hated it. But I've finally figured out it was because my body knew his, knew who he was supposed to be. And now my soul is drawn just as strongly to you," she told him.

He kissed her again, chastely, pulling away before she could reach for him. Catching her seeking hands, he held them still and shook his head. "You don't need another round right now, darlin'. And we need to get back on the road before your honor guard comes looking for us. They still don't trust me.

"Eilrah says we should reach your village mid-day tomorrow," he murmured, rubbing his gritty eyes absently. His mouth tightened briefly as he imagined what a fiasco that was going to be. Her villagers had no doubt heard tales of her promised warrior, and probably hated him as much as Eiona had hated Rue.

He helped her gently to her feet and watched as she gingerly moved around with the toy in her butt, slowly at first, and then more gracefully, more easily as her body accustomed itself to the foreign invasion. "If that's hurting you, we will take it out," he offered as she slowly started to don her clothes.

She cast him a slow smile over one smooth shoulder and said, "One of the benefits of being a priestess. My body doesn't feel pain for long, and it heals unbelievably quickly." She bent over to pick up her borrowed breeches, and Kye groaned as the movement spread the rounded cheeks of her butt, giving him a long, taunting look at the ruby device she had nestled in her ass.

"Witch," he muttered, shaking his head and reaching for his clothes.

She laughed and came up behind him, pressing her clothed body to his naked one and wrapping her arms around him. "It's only a day, sweet. We can use it to see how good our control is," she teased, rising on her toes to press a kiss to his neck. He felt the hot brush of her lips, felt a puff of air as she spoke and he had to stifle a groan.

When it came to Eiona, he had no control.

None.

Zero.

Zippo.

And she knew it, damn her. She left the clearing, casting a smoky, hot look at him just before disappearing around a curve in the trail.

Kye paused long enough after he donned his clothes to pin the dragon with an evil look. "Enjoy yourself?" he asked sarcastically.

Eilrah laughed, the deep bass of it echoing in Kye's chest, as the dragon purred, "Absolutely. Didn't you, every time you watched as she pleasured her man?"

Kye's neck reddened and he felt the blush moving up his face. He drawled out, "There's a bit of a difference. You put me in that place, kept me from being able to leave, from doing any damn thing. I had no choice but to watch. I can't say I didn't enjoy it, but I didn't have a choice either way."

"You, on the other hand, did."

He turned and stalked away, pausing only briefly when the dragon said, "There is yet another difference, young Kye. My kind sees no harm in taking pleasure in watching our bonded priestess and her warrior mate. That you find it disagreeable is your failing."

Kye flipped the voyeuristic dragon off, uncertain if he knew what the gesture meant, but it sure as hell made him feel better.

Bad enough he got yanked into this world. Eilrah can just handle that.

And he had a feeling he was falling, seriously and hard, for Eiona.

But what did he do to deserve a mouthy, arrogant, know it all *dragon*?

* * * * *

He dreamed that night.

Not of Eiona.

But of Ashlyn.

God, he had loved her. There was a part of him that would always belong to her.

But he knew he couldn't ever go back to her.

Even if Eilrah said it was possible, Kye couldn't go back. Something inside him had changed. There was something dark inside him now, something that would keep them from the happiness they had once shared.

But it hurt.

In the dream, he seemed to stand on the sidelines, wearing his warrior's clothes, watching little snippets of their life. Watching as they met for the first time, watching as she pretended to let him seduce her, watching as they married, as they made love for the first time as man and wife.

And those brief hours he had shared her with Connor.

He felt himself moving through his dream, walking closer to them, watching them from his new body. The larger, broader Kye lifted a hand and pressed it against the barrier that separated them.

Morning came, and he woke feeling more confused than ever.

And torn.

* * * * *

A day later, Kye was certain he was going insane.

His heart felt like one raw, oozing bruise and his head ached.

On the other hand, his body was tight and hot from unrelieved sexual frustration the likes of which he had never known.

His cock wasn't certain how much more of this he could take.

Kye didn't know how much more he could take.

His cock had been standing at raging attention for the past three hours, when four young *very* nubile women had led Eiona into a central area at the village.

First they had stripped her.

Then they had laid her body on mats and tended what few injuries remained.

After that a long bath in one of the hot springs that bubbled out of the ground, hidden from sight as they led her into the shelter around the spring. Some drifted away, others remained.

When she was led back out, Kye had closed his eyes and whispered a ragged, "Fuck."

She was naked.

And her mound had been waxed smooth again.

By the look in her eyes, she had done that with him in mind.

Then the massage.

Hell, the massage.

Every inch of her gleaming, pale gold body was oiled and slicked and rubbed. Her neck, arms, and torso. Then her legs from instep to hip. And finally they spread her legs and oiled the naked plump lips that guarded her sex, oiled the soft flesh there until it gleamed. And every bloody man in the village seemed to be watching.

Including Kar and Eagan.

The few who could tear their eyes from Eiona's body would send him evil, assessing glares. Kye had to wonder if he was going to wake up one night, very soon, with a knife in his gut.

But the women were worse. Because not a one of them seemed interested in Eiona and every single one, from the women Eiona's age to the gray haired women, seemed to be studying and grading him.

He could ignore them, as long as he focused on something else.

And Eiona was the something else.

Right now, they were painting her nipples with a creamy reddish pink paint that matched the folds of her sex. Kye had to clench his fists and count to fifty to keep from grabbing somebody's cloak and covering that long naked body.

When they rolled her onto her belly, he stiffened.

Strong slender hands worked the muscles in her back. Another pair of hands poured more of the sweet, warm oil on her back, until her flesh gleamed in the pale lavender light.

Eilrah sat holding court. Or judging the ritual, whatever the dragon wanted to call it. Kye couldn't take the cold, evil, angry glares coming at him from his back so he moved to the dragon, unaware of the gasps and starts his actions caused.

Eagan and Kar moved to join them, flanking him. Kye was surprised to feel the mutual support coming from each of them, especially young Eagan. The young man glanced at him, forgoing the deferential dropping of his eyes. "Rue Abulein sought only to cause pain, to all around him. He would never have sought to give the lady pleasure."

"You've given them something to think about, Kye," Eilrah added.

"Huh?"

"The unclean of soul rarely dare approach a dragon. And never one bonded to a priestess. We tend to gut those who force themselves on us," Eilrah said, still watching the crowd.

Guarding me, Kye realized with a start.

"Aye. I am afraid you will need guarding here for a time. Until they realize you are no threat to them or Eiona." He cast Kye a glance and lowered his voice even more to whisper, "Put your hand on my wing, mortal."

Kye pulled back, staring at the dragon, his hungry perusal of Eiona forgotten. His eyes dropped to the leathery black wings, each one bigger than his body. Each one could spread wide and each one sported nasty claws at the apex, like an extra hand—long, wicked claws.

I don't *think so,* Kye thought warily.

"Your hand, Kye. On my wing," he repeated. "Dragons do not like to be touched by anybody but those they bond with. To do so without permission means only one of two things. Either you are very foolish, or you are one the dragon calls friend."

Kar said quietly, "Not one of the villagers would dare to touch the lady's *Orinduuc*, warrior. They fear the great lizards too much, fear them almost as much as they respect them."

Slowly, hesitantly, Kye lifted one hand. He laid his palm on the wing, feeling it hot and smooth, more like a silk sheet than a leathery appendage. "Do I have to ask which one I am?" he asked half seriously, ignoring the muffled gasps around him as he absently stroked up the wing to rest his hand on Eilrah's neck.

"Well, I do not know. Friend. Do you?" Eilrah asked, arching his neck and humming with pleasure when Kye started to rub around the base of one of his neck spines with an absent, certain touch.

"I still think one of them is going to try pissing in my soup," he muttered, shaking his head before turning his eyes back to Eiona. "I really do not know how much more of this I can handle. Shit, why can't I do that?" He heard the plaintive note in his voice as oiled hands massaged and stroked Eiona's gleaming body.

"If you chose to, you could. But you've a dislike of mating in public and I doubt you could keep from mounting her," Eilrah replied with a smug dragon laugh.

"You had no trouble mounting her in front of me," Eagan said wryly. "Why not mount her here and now?"

Kye sent the younger man a withering glance. "Aren't you supposed to be afraid of me?"

Kar laughed as Eagan tried to sputter out a denial. "You shared your woman, warrior. You do not share your woman with somebody you consider unworthy. He is your equal. You made him so."

Eilrah snorted in agreement and silently added, *Elai usually take on a young man to train, a second body guard for the priestess. Some one to take into their household, as a brother. You might as well acknowledge him.*

Take that brat into his house?

Eilrah laughed, a deep chuffing sound in his throat. Kye tried hard to ignore him. Of course, that let him focus on Eiona and the crowd even more.

"Why does this have to be public?" He *really* didn't like all these other men staring at that toned, sleek body.

"Because this is their day. They have their priestess back," Eilrah answered. "They haven't had a priestess since Eiona's mother died, nearly a decade ago. Normally, one priestess takes another in training once she has established herself, but Esme was called home before she could start training Eiona. And for a very long time, it looked as though Eiona wasn't going to have her mother's gifts, even though they paid for the training."

"They paid for her training, for her supplies, and will continue to do so. Having her here is good for them, she will bless their crops, protect them from the wild magicks in the beyond, and keep the balance. But her training didn't come cheap. Raising her was something that they all paid for. And now, today, they get a little of that back.

"And I'm sure a good many of the villagers are almost as disgusted that they will see no fucking as they are about her bonding with you. When she came back from Aspberal without you and joined with Aiken, they all assumed Rue would be her *elai*, but never her lover, never her mate. They have heard of Rue, I am sure you know. And seeing her with you causes them uneasy moments. But they will see, as she did."

Uneasy.

Oh, so that was it.

The malice he felt directed at him was because they were uneasy.

Yeah, right.

Kar's weathered hand landed on his shoulder and the older man squeezed. "Give it time, Kye. I know not what has happened, but I see a different man inside your eyes. They will see it as well."

He hadn't expected the villagers to take their turns at him as well. A little warning would have been nice. But he was led from his borrowed lodge late the next morning, so late the sun was already nearing its zenith. Led out by four very broad, very powerful looking men, out into the crowd and stripped by impersonal hands. If Eilrah hadn't warned him with a simple shake of his spined head, Kye would have gotten pretty damn nasty at that time.

But he saw the head shake.

Knew what it meant.

And just hoped he wouldn't have *men* rubbing him down.

Eagan stayed by his side without being asked, silent and stoic, and Kye resigned himself to taking the man as whatever in the hell Eilrah had suggested. He was taken to one of the bathing houses and stepped into one of the deeper pools before they could throw him.

With a sigh of bliss, he sank into the warm, bubbling water. A faint metallic scent stung the air, overlain with fragrant burning candles.

This was the first peaceful moment he had been given since he had entered into the crazy world.

Of course, why wasn't he surprised when it didn't last.

Eagan dropped to the side of the pool, politely staring into the empty space ahead of him and said, "You need your hair washed. If I were you, I'd get it done before they decide to."

Kye scowled and went under, wetting his hair and holding out a hand for whatever he needed to wash it with.

Later, clad only in his wet hair and pale hide, he was led from the tent into the center square by the same four men. Eagan was once more silently at his back as Kye trailed after the solemn and silent villagers.

If the dragon expected Kye to allow men to rub him down...

He heaved a sigh of relief when the same four women from the previous day rounded the corner, Eiona in their wake, clad in a white robe that reminded him of ancient Greece and togas, cords crisscrossed between her breasts, under them, while the skirt fell in sheer folds around her thighs, slit up both sides to mid thigh.

Once he had lain down on the warmed stone, Eagan left his side and took a place just behind Eiona, and the people around him allowed it, as if they knew he had a place there.

He forced his mind to blank.

But he couldn't do it once they started with the massage.

The oils were warm, tauntingly, erotically warm and his cock jerked to life in heartbeats. Hell, had Eiona felt this? Maybe not. After all, it had been women bathing her, rubbing her down, maybe that wasn't such an erotic experience for another woman.

Then he met her eyes across the distance that separated them and thought, *Not*. She had been turned on by it, just as she was being turned on by them now. As he stared into her eyes, he felt the gentle brush of her soul on his, felt her tugging on his consciousness just before she whispered silently to him,

Are you certain you do not wish to mate with me until nightfall? Can your body truly stand twelve more hours of this?

Kye wasn't certain he could stand it.

But it had been bad enough being stripped in front of a bunch of strangers. Fucking in front of them?

Not goingto happen, babe.

Her mouth curved up in a sweet, taunting smile and Kye stifled a groan. She was going to make this hell.

The hands continued to stroke and glide over him, but he could no longer even pretend there was some therapeutic value in this. Not when the hands lingered and caressed his backside, not when slim fingers would stray between his buttocks, or glide down to cup his balls.

He lay on his stomach, his cock burning into his belly, aching and throbbing. Then the hands started to turn him over. He resisted momentarily, before realizing just how stupid that would make him look. He suspected the whole point of this exercise was to get him hard, so it wasn't like he was keeping any secret from them.

Now lying on his back, his cock was straining upward, pulsating with every beat of his heart, the cool air brushing over him like the softest caress. He resisted the impulse to look at the handmaidens who continued to work and caress his body, instead closing his eyes and trying to pretend he was elsewhere.

But they weren't making it easy.

His breath hissed out from between his teeth when a hand closed boldly around his cock, gripping it and stroking it with a milking massage, spreading the warmed oil over his flesh and driving him nearer insanity.

Still certain?

His eyes flew open and he stared into Eiona's gaze. She was the one fondling his cock and balls, while the other women massaged and kneaded the muscles in his thighs.

Witch, he mouthed up at her, shuddering as her teasing hands continued to pump his cock, slowly, firmly, until he didn't give a damn that nearly a hundred people were watching her give him a hand job. His lids dropped, blocking out the sight of her in her lovely, sexy little gown, the sight of other feminine hands moving over his flesh.

He was going to come. All over her hand, all over himself, in front of all these people. He lifted his lids slowly, and stared up into her eyes. *Stop, Eiona,* he mouthed, narrowing his eyes at her and thinking the same words as hard as he could.

She lifted her chin in acknowledgement before giving his aching shaft one last stroke. She moved until she was by his head, dropping to her knees and resting her chin on the warmed slab of stone where he lay. "Such a shy man you are, Kye," she murmured, staring into his eyes.

"Just because I choose not to fuck in front of other people doesn't mean I'm shy," he answered. "I noticed you took out that little toy Eilrah gave you before you were brought out here yesterday. Does that make you shy?"

She lifted a brow and replied, "Excellent point." Staring down the length of his body, she judged and said, "They will be done soon. How do you feel?"

"Like my dick's about to explode," he replied wryly.

She laughed and rose. "Save that for me, if you please. Last chance. Sure you want to wait?"

He groaned and demanded, "Just get this over with before I lose it right here."

He was led away from her and clothed in flowing silken breeches. They were the color of burgundy wine — nearly the same color as his hair — topped with an open vest embroidered with ivory and gold thread. He wasn't given any shoes and when he asked, the girl just smiled and went for his hair, combing out the braid he had bound it in after the bath, brushing it until it gleamed.

And of course, when he tried to shove it back out of his face and back into a loose tail, he got his hand smacked. The youngest of the girls stared nervously at him after the eldest did so, her eyes full of fear and panic. He closed his eyes and sighed.

He didn't like having people look at him with fear.

Didn't like having men look at him in disgust and women refuse to meet his eyes. Or worse, even cross his path.

He was led back outside and met Eilrah on the path. "Are these people ever going to trust me?" he asked gruffly. As he spoke, a child barreled out of his lodge, careening towards him. Automatically Kye knelt and caught him as his mother tried to catch up, and he stared down into the large, sweet eyes of innocence. One hand reached up to brush at his hair while the other grabbed for the shiny threads on his vest.

His heart clenched painfully as memories started to run through his mind. And dreams he wasn't certain he would ever get to see happen.

"Babies always smell sweet, so innocent," he murmured. "We were going to have a lot of them, Ash and me. Eventually."

"So sorry, milord, so sorry," the woman babbled rushing up to them, her eyes full of tears, fear, and anxiety. And the urge to protect.

With a sigh, Kye turned to baby over and snapped, "I wasn't about to eat him, lady. I didn't want him to fall."

He looked away from her, and the sweet little boy-child and stared at Eilrah. His turbulent mind was driving him near insane. He had to get away from here for a little while and think.

"I need to be alone, dragon. I have to think," he whispered tightly. The dream from the past night was circling through his brain, interspersed with random memories from this new life.

Eiona, masturbating by the river and offering him a taste.

Ashlyn throwing herself at him with laughter in her eyes.

The car barreling out of nowhere and shattering his body.

The pain.

Watching as Ashlyn and Connor both suffered through the months after the death of his old body.

Eiona and her lover Aiken, first loving wildly and passionately. And then Aiken dead and Eiona hovering over his lifeless body.

"I need to be alone," he repeated.

With a gusty sigh that smelled of hot stones and fire, Eilrah rested his head on his fore-claws and said, "Then go."

Kye turned on his bare heel and stalked away.

While Eilrah watched the confused frightened woman disappear into her lodge, child held tightly to her chest, he sighed again, long plumes of smoke coming from his nares.

"This," he mourned, "is not going to be easy."

Kye stood at the edge of the forest, staring down the hill into the village. He felt naked and it took a long time for him to figure out why.

No weapons.

He had already gotten so accustomed to them that he felt naked without the sword, his throwing knives, numerous other blades, and his bow.

He was so confused.

He felt torn. Part of him yearned for home and Ashlyn.

The other part knew he was no longer the one for her, and no longer the person she had known. Hell, he didn't even know himself right now.

And he couldn't imagine leaving Eiona.

Or Eilrah.

He sat, falling back and resting his back against a trunk with bark that felt abnormally smooth. Closing his eyes, he fell back into sleep and back into the dream that had made no sense.

But this time, when he reached out to touch the barrier, Ashlyn rolled over and climbed from her bed. Connor remained sleeping, unaware. The words, when she spoke, sounded and felt almost foreign to Kye.

"I am fine, Kye. I am happy."

"I miss you," he said gruffly. "Miss everything about you."

She smiled, sadly. "I miss you, too. But this is my life now. And you have yours. Go live it."

"Aren't I dead?" he asked. This felt weird.

Too weird.

And too real.

"I don't think you are," she said, her smooth naked shoulders lifting in a shrug. "Go. Live. Connor will take care of me. He will keep me happy."

"That was supposed to be my job," Kye joked weakly.

Ashlyn reached up, laid her palm next to his, and pushed. Slowly her hand passed through the barrier until she could fold it around his. "Yes. For a while, it was. And you did it well. I will always love you, Kye. But we are over."

He felt the throb of her pulse in her palm. Slowly, he leaned in, drawing her closer. The barrier thinned, wavered and disappeared altogether for a moment, leaving them suspended in between their worlds as Kye pressed his lips gently to Ashlyn's.

A cool metal chain was wrapped around his wrist and when he broke contact to look down, the barrier came back and he could just barely see Ashlyn as it started to solidify. In his hand, he held a golden chain, one he had given Ashlyn, a Celtic knot. His grandmother had given it to him before she died and he had given it to Ashlyn the night they married. She had been wearing it since then—Kye wondered, with a brief smirk, what Connor thought of that.

"Be happy," she whispered, an echo of the words he had told her months earlier. "I need to know you will be."

He nodded slowly. "Good bye, Ash."

"Good bye, Kye," she whispered.

And the barrier clouded over and blackened.

Kye awoke to feel a tiny hand shaking his shoulder.

He stared up into a young expectant face. As he sat up, something fell from his hand. Ignoring the girl, he reached down and lifted the golden charm and chain, watching as the sunlight glinted off of it.

"Did you find what you needed?" the girl asked softly, sitting down next to him and looking at the charm.

"Yeah," he said, his voice tight and hoarse. "Yeah. I think I did." He let the charm fall on the chain—watched as it swung and glinted in the sun—before he put it around his neck. The charm settled in the hollow of his throat and he remembered the day his grandmother had given it to him. Kye had never been to Ireland, had only gone to see her weeks before she died. He had spent nearly a month there, depressed and morose, and Connor had finally flown in from the States— where he had been going to college—to bring him home.

He touched the tiny charm and smiled slowly, remembering the towering cliffs, the rocky beaches again. He had gone back nearly every summer after that—usually to spend time with Connor—but sometimes alone. Now he had something else of home besides his memories.

* * * * *

Eilrah couldn't decide whether he was happy about being wrong, or disgusted because he was wrong.

Dragons really did hate to be wrong.

Kye had gone missing.

So had a young, very promising witch, a child of only nine who had the gifts of future sight and soul-seeing. She was likely to go beyond being even a priestess, maybe even serving on the Witches Council.

The one with the gift of soul seeing could do what Eiona could do with a touch, her bare flesh on another's. Seeing inside the soul, inside the heart. But Rianne didn't need to touch. She had only to look.

When she was three an odd white wolven appeared outside the lodge where she played, and the wolven never left. It was her first familiar, one the wise men didn't even realize she had summoned.

Her gift had emerged early, surprising even the wise men who looked for the latent gifts. From the time she was four, all she had to do was simply look at a person. For months, she was safe, seeing things that her young mind didn't understand, but nothing that caused her pain, until one day when a trader came into the village, selling herbs, spices, metals, and cloth.

Rianne had taken one look at him and screamed. And the wolven started to growl and bay outside the man's wagon.

The nightmares had taken months to fade.

The wise men had ordered him seized, and while four strong, powerful young hunters held him, the two wise men searched the wagon. Rianne's young wolven leaped into the wagon, clawing at the floor boards until they found something ghastly.

An odd group of memoirs. A severed hand, child sized, a bloody shift, many locks of hair, leather and metal bindings, and gold. Gold from the north, sent to the trader in exchange for the last trio of children he had sold them.

Not just a slaver, but a child murderer as well.

Rianne couldn't be in the presence of evil, not at her age. Until she was able to train her gifts and learn the basics of shielding, she was to be protected, and so was sent away to the southern schools where the witches were trained. She came home on holidays and two or three weeks in the summer, when most of the traders were closer to the borderlands, gathering the supplies they would sell the coming winter.

This was one of those few summer breaks, and normally she was inseparable from her parents.

But she had gone missing, right at the same time Kye stormed out of the village in his festive finery.

The searchers found them by the lazily flowing river, Rianne curled up in Kye's lap, listening wide-eyed to the stories of buiken that had horns and flew through the sky while pulling a wheel-less wagon filled with toys, driven by a man with white beard and kind, twinkling eyes. And snow.

Right now, the child couldn't imagine which one sounded more joyous. The toys. Or the snow.

It was the youngest wise man who stared in wonder before turning to look at Eiona who rode at the tail of the search party, on her borrowed rean. She could have told them exactly where Kye was, but she was a little too angry with them. Even if they couldn't trust Kye, they should have been able to trust her.

Kye barely even glanced at his audience, instead wrapping up his story and listening to the pretty little girl as she wished to see snow and flying reindeer. And then the little girl bussed his cheeks gently before standing and staring at the crowd with solemn eyes.

"I have to go," she said with a sigh. "My silly mama is worrying. She shouldn't, though. You're better now, are you not?"

Kye smiled slightly and said, "Yeah. Yes, my little lady, I am better."

Kye watched as she headed back down the trail, following her slowly, ignoring the men around him. When he was at Eiona's side, he stared up at her and held out his hand.

She slid from the rean's back and took his hand, walking with him along the trail back into the village.

She waited until they had passed out of sight of the villagers before tugging them off the trail and turning to study him with troubled eyes. She lifted a finger to touch the golden piece that rested in the hollow of his throat. "I've seen this before," she said quietly, fighting not to pout.

"It belonged to my grandmother," Kye said, resisting the urge to roll his eyes and sigh. He reached up and covered her hand, holding it in place. "She gave it to me before she died and I gave it to Ash. I...I saw her just now—*How in the fuck did I see her?*—she gave it back."

Eiona's eyes were dark, sulky. "Your grandmother?"

"My father's mother," he said. "I know that's the right word for it. I am speaking your tongue, woman and you understand me. You even know I'm telling the truth. You just don't like it. It..." his words trailed off and he lifted her hand to his mouth, pressing his lips to it before he turned away, studying the foreign trees, the foreign land. Even the sky was bizarre, with its lavender color and the clouds that blazed red.

"I would not leave you, even if I were given the choice, Eiona." His fingers went up to touch the charm at his neck and his voice went rough with emotion as he said, "This is home."

Chapter Ten

ဢ

No. Eiona admitted to herself later. She didn't like it. At all. It was a pretty piece of work — exotic, foreign, lovely. If she had seen a merchant selling such a piece, she would have bought it greedily.

She didn't like it because Kye had given it to another woman. Kye had loved another woman.

And nothing she did would ever change that.

So she had simply reached up and kissed first him, then the golden piece and asked what it meant. *A Celtic knot.* What ever that meant. Afterward she shoved it — very forcefully — to the back of her mind. It hadn't been a gift from another woman, after all. It had belonged to Kye, first. Well, his blood family, first.

* * * * *

Eiona stared into the mirror at her reflection.

She might as well be naked, and would probably be more comfortable that way.

The gown they had put her in was nearly translucent, showing the darker flesh of her nipples, and the shadowed cleft between her thighs. When she moved, the dim light shown through and highlighted each limb.

Her body was aching.

A slow, pulsing throb passed through her loins as she heard him outside.

Tonight she would become his mate, in name and action, as well as soul. This man she had only known for weeks, who had been thrown so violently into her world.

She passed a hand through her short cap of curls, the ends floating down to caress her neck. She wanted it long again, wanted to wear it around her as a cloak and taunt and tease Kye with it.

When he came through the door, she forgot all about anything else. He stood staring at her—bare-chested, his golden charm lying against his throat, wearing only the loose flowing breeches he had worn when the wise man had bound their wrists with flowered vines. His long, silken hair spilled over his wide shoulders as he moved closer to her, the muscles in his flat belly rippling. Each now wore a gold cuff on the right wrist—a symbol of that binding. She had driven their craftsmen mad when she had given them an extra chore—to carve his cuff with a series of those knots—echoing the charm he wore. A tiny smile had curved his wide, sensuous mouth and she had seen his pleasure—so it had been worth it, indeed

His breeches were silky and slung low on his narrow hips, caressing the thick ridge of his cock.

Eiona trailed her eyes down the length of his body, lingering on the bulge of his sex, before moving back up to his face. Her breath caught in her throat at what she saw there.

His eyes were hot.

She felt the near palpable caress of his eyes as they ran over her body and she smiled, turning to face him. The device in her bottom stung slightly as she walked over to him. Rising on her toes, she linked her arms around his neck and whispered, "Do you know our traditions? After the bonding ceremony, we are left alone for three days and nights. My handmaidens will bring us food, your second will come with them and bring wood for the fire, fresh clothing and linens.

"But we are totally alone," she murmured against his mouth. "And before we leave this lodge, I will feel this inside my bottom." She cupped him in her hand and hummed low in her throat as he started to rock against her touch, the slick material of his breeches sliding easily across his flesh as she caressed him.

His hand trailed over her side, around to cup her bottom before seeking and finding the dildo lodged in her backside. He pressed against it rhythmically as he lowered his head to kiss her sweet mouth.

She shuddered as he started to caress her aching body. The diaphanous gown fell away under his hand, baring her body to him. Her nipples tightened unbearably and she cried out when he lifted her up so that he could feast on them. Moments later, she was on her back, on a mound of pillows piled in front of the fire.

Kye settled back on his heels and spread her thighs, tracing his fingers down the naked flesh of her mound, flicking her a glance as he murmured, "Such a pretty little sight you are, naked and wet and waiting for me." He petted her gently, teasingly, until she cried out in frustration. The bared flesh was smooth and silken soft, and when he spread her apart, the reddened flesh of her sex gleamed wetly. Lowering his body, he held her open with his fingers and stroked her with his tongue. "Tasty, too. So sweet."

She screamed when he stiffened his tongue and buried it inside her, laving the inner walls of her sex, nuzzling her clit, while his hand trailed down until he could press against the sex toy buried inside her ass. "Fill me, please," she begged, reaching for him, lifting her hips in need.

"What's the hurry?" he teased, even though he was half out of his mind already, so deep was his need.

"I need to feel you inside me. Don't tease me, not tonight," she whimpered. She cried out when he thrust two fingers inside her wet aching passage as he started to move higher up her body.

He waited until she was creaming in his hand, until the spasms of climax were tightening her body and then he freed his cock and drove deep inside, burying himself to the balls while she screamed and bucked beneath him. She was clamped tightly around him, more than normal, thanks to the toy they hadn't removed.

A rumbling groan tore from his throat as she whimpered and squirmed, her body adjusting to the deep, near painful fit of his cock inside her. He held still, waiting in agony, until the walls of her sheath stopped shuddering endlessly, waited until her breathing slowed.

And then he started to pump. Deep and slow, until she opened her dazed eyes and stared up at him. Once she was looking at him, he grabbed her hands and pinned her down, fucking her hard and fast and deep, groaning when he felt the walls of her sex fluttering around his cock.

He moved higher, angling his hips so that each hard, deep dig rubbed his cock head against the rich bed of nerves deep in her channel. When she stiffened and shoved against him, eyes wide as the pleasure bordered on pain, he drove inside her harder, resisting her half hearted attempts to pull her hands free.

When she was pleading and crying against him, he stopped.

She was teetering on the very edge as he turned her over and lifted her hips in his big hands. He stroked his cock through the wet well of her sex, pressing the pad of his thumb against the base of the toy in her ass to drive it deeper inside her ass as he rode her. Angling her hips high, he steadied her and started to work his cock back inside her.

She was swollen, clamping down tight as she neared orgasm, and Kye had to work his length into her slowly. By the time he seated himself fully in her creamy, wet depths, his chest was shuddering with ragged breaths and she was beginning to come around him.

He gritted his teeth and rode it out and when she fell limply down, he started to shaft her, keeping her ass open and high with his hands. With slow steady thrusts, he rode her, judging her reactions, and adjusting his pace to them. When he pushed her hips down just a little, it made her back stiffen and arch. As he reached out to pinch her clit, she mewled and shoved back against him. And every time he brushed the dildo even slightly, she went wild around him, thrashing and shoving her butt tightly against him.

Eiona could hardly breathe and her vision shifted and swirled before her, but she couldn't stop pleading for more. His hand left her butt and lifted high, coming down with a resounding smack on her ass that had her screaming. Again, and again, Kye slapped her ass and the fire started to burn uncontrollably— spreading from the hot area on her ass to her clit, to her womb and outward, cream flooding from her passage with a wet gush as she came— clenching around him so hard, coming so hard, her vision grayed, then blackened.

Kye fell against her with a cry as he flooded her welcoming body with his seed, keeping her tightly pressed against him as he rolled to his side. Turning to his back and snagging a fur throw from the floor, he tugged it over them, then buried his face in her short locks, and fell into sleep.

She woke to feel his gentle hands cleaning his seed from her body. She purred and stretched under his touch and reached for him only to have him shake his head, eying her with solemn eyes. "I have an agenda," he told her seriously, a tiny smile curling one corner of his mouth.

"An agenda?" she repeated, the word unfamiliar on her tongue, sounding flat to her ears.

"Where I was born, an agenda means your plan for the day. Well, night. And I have an agenda."

"What is this...agenda?" she asked, gasping as he pressed the cloth just inside her, rubbing lightly before retreating. He tossed it aside and reached for another, repeating the same steps until she was fairly certain her nether regions were as clean as they could possibly be.

Well, she still had the dildo. It made her gasp as he shifted her body, forcing it into a different, and very pleasing, angle.

"Feed me. I'm starving," he murmured, taking another cloth and another bowl of clear, warm, scented water and washing her breasts, her stiff nipples, and her torso.

She looked at him, disappointed, but he wasn't looking at her face.

"Famished," he continued gruffly, lowering his head and nipping sharply at one peaked nipple. "And you're on the menu. Matter of fact, you are the menu. I'm going to clean your body up and then taste every last inch of you. And then I plan on you doing the same to me."

Her lids fluttered closed and she whispered, "Sounds lovely." Her words faded to a moan as he started to circle her clit with his thumb. He nibbled his way from her tits down to her navel and on to the naked lips of her sex, laving the plump, soft flesh with his tongue before turning his attention to the throbbing flesh of her clitoris, standing stiff and swollen.

She cried out when he licked it lazily, and screamed when he took it between his teeth and pulled. And then she started swearing at him, because he had pulled away and turned her onto her belly. He laughed as she glared at him and said, "Have to stick to the agenda. Which means cleaning every last inch so I can taste every last inch." Lowering his head, he whispered into her ear as he started to draw the plug from her ass, "And sometime before we leave this lodge, I'm going to fuck every orifice you have."

Dropping down, he kissed the tender, sore flesh of her rosette, circling it with his tongue before reaching for another rag.

By the time Kye judged her body to be suitably clean, she was groaning and half laughing and swearing in frustration. Baths were generally just to clean, could be sensual, but had never turned her into a thing of heated, burning need that cried and pleaded to be fucked.

She reached for him, wrapping his long hair around her hands and tugging, trying to pull him up to cover her. He came willingly enough, since she had a death grip on his hair, but as soon as she released the dark-red locks, he caught her hands, and shot to his feet. He padded over to the bag he had brought in with him and drew out several lengths of red silk.

"I want to tie you up," he told her warningly. "If you tell me no, right now, I'll forget it. But there's quite a bit I want to do with your body and you're not letting me do it my way."

She eyed the silken scarves nervously, her mind briefly flitting back to the months she had spent in bondage. But more than the memories, her mind was crowded with the image of him doing what he wanted to her. Along the bond they shared, she caught images and thought of just what he wanted, how he wanted to do it, and knew it would be nothing but pleasure.

She saw his eyes widen with surprise as she lay down and lifted arms over her head, placing them, incidentally, right next to a heavy table carved from brusa stone. When he straddled her body and started to bind her, he wrapped the length of red silk around the massive table leg first, and then looped it over her wrists.

The position he had taken put his enormous cock just within mouth's reach and Eiona hummed with pleasure before drawing her tongue up that long, pulsating shaft once. Then she took the fat, flared head into her mouth and started to suck.

Kye groaned and shifted slightly, enabling him to thrust his cock into her mouth. "Was gonna save that particular orifice for later," he muttered. "But since you insist." He took handfuls of her short silky hair and moved her head in a different rhythm. "I'm going to come inside your mouth, baby. Then we'll get on with the agenda."

He thrust deep, and she gently locked her teeth, holding him inside as she slowly forced the muscles in her throat to relax and unbelievably, she took him almost all the way down until the need for air made her pull back. He relented briefly and then drove in again, pushing his cock past her lips, through her mouth and moaning as he slid down her throat.

The muscles in his long, powerful body clenched and tightened, sweat starting to bead lightly on his body, as she took him deep inside, the silken walls of her mouth and throat driving him insane. His lids drooped, his dark eyes nearly blind with need as the orgasm ripped through him.

Hot, pulsing jets of sperm flooded from him, down her throat but he continued to pump in and out, fucking her mouth with something akin to desperation, his flesh still hard and rigid. "Deeper, baby, can you take it just a little deeper?" he panted, releasing her hair and leaning, forward propping his hands on the stone table.

The muscles in his arms bunched and flexed as he moved over her, driving his cock deeper into her mouth. Eiona pulled back, as far as she could in her bound position and he acquiesced, pulling his stiff member from her mouth, his eyes dark with need and hunger and just a slight touch of disappointment. Eiona ignored it, concentrated on drawing air into lungs and then blanked her mind, took a control of her body that was so minute, she could have willed her heart to slow if she so chose.

Slowly she started to lick at his member and when he pushed past her lips, she held her breath and waited. First the back of her mouth, then she could feel the head of his cock in her throat, and finally, she could take no more but nearly nine of his ten thick inches were inside her. Helplessly, he bucked and thrust against her until he came again.

With a ragged sigh, he forced himself to move off her and listened as she gasped air into her starving lungs. Holy shit, she had nearly swallowed him completely down. He hadn't ever felt anything like that before.

He should have been empty. Hell, he'd come in her sweet mouth twice, in only a handful of minutes.

But once his breathing slowed and his heart regulated, his twitching cock flared back to rampant and hungry life.

With a gleam in his eyes, he spread her thighs and used the last of his two silken ropes to tie her legs apart, one to a large iron basket meant to hold fire wood, the other to a heavy lounge.

Glancing up at her, he said, "Get ready." He sprawled between her widespread legs, lifted her ass in his hands and buried his face against her bare mound.

It was nearly an hour before he left off eating her dripping, throbbing cleft. Taking his cock in hand, he propped himself over her bound body and started to work his way into her. Her flesh was so sensitized by now, it was nearly painful just to take him inside.

"You're tight," he whispered. "Sweet, wet, and so fucking tight."

Eiona mewled weakly beneath him, pinioned down, unable to move as he worked the head of his fat cock inside her. She shuddered and clamped down convulsively and he groaned above her. "Damn it, baby, don't do that," he growled.

"Please, please, please, please," she cried, thrashing her head back and forth.

"So tight. So tiny," he crooned, lowering his head to kiss her trembling mouth. "Please what? Am I hurting you? Do you want me to stop?" He made to withdraw and she cried out plaintively, which had him burrowing back inside her. "Or are you asking me to fuck you?"

"Damn it, Kye," she hissed, trying to rock her hips upward.

"Fuck you? Or quit?"

"Don't you stop, don't you dare, please," she gasped when he surged forward, sliding three more inches of hot, satin smooth cock inside her wet sheath.

He settled on his knees, pulling out and she swore at him. But he was only freeing her legs. The silk scarves came loose from their moorings and she quickly drew her legs up, locking them around his hips and jerking him forward.

He laughed, grinning down at her, asking, "In a hurry?"

Jerking on her wrists, she said, "Free my hands."

A slow, masculine smile spread across Kye's face and he shook his head, staring down at her. Her arms were still tied, wrists together, bound to the stout stone table leg. Her spine arched, lifting her full, round breasts upward, her nipples red and hard as berries. Her flat belly quivered with every breath as she lifted her hips, trying to draw him inside her.

He stared at the naked mound of her sex, her gleaming folds spread wide, red, swollen and dripping with cream.

"No," he mused, taking his cock in his hand and aiming for those pouting lips that guarded her sex, slowing surging forward, watching as she took his engorged cock into her eager body. "You look good like this, open and ready for me. So...fuckable," he decided, as he slid further inside her. On his knees, holding her hips in his hands, he used his upper body strength to pull her further down on his cock until he was seated all the way inside, until his balls would sway forward to brush against her ass every time he drove home.

Dropping forward, he draped her legs over his arms, holding her open, keeping her ass high, her legs spread wide. Then he hunched over her bound body and proceeded to fuck her hard, bringing pleas and cries to her lips. Leaning over her, he whispered against her mouth, "Say my name when you come. I wanna hear it when you come around me."

"Kye," she gasped, struggling to move. But she was immobile, her hands still bound. And with her butt lifted, her legs spread wide and draping over Kye's arms, she had no leverage. She shuddered as he buried himself at her core, repeatedly. She could feel the thick ridge of his cock, the head caressing the rich bed of nerves buried high in her passage,

122

and each thrust had him pressing against the mouth of her womb.

Each dig of his cock shoved her closer to the edge, where she bordered between pleasure and pain. He lowered his body, until he was rubbing against her swollen clit and that contact sent her screaming into orgasm, her vaginal walls closing around his cock and tightening like a wet, greedy fist that milked the seed from his body in hot pulsating jets. And she screamed out his name when she came.

* * * * *

Sometime while they slept, the handmaidens delivered food and clothes, very minimal clothes, while the men carried in a very large copper tub, which was filled with water for them to use once they woke.

Excellent timing, was all Kye could think when he woke less than a half hour after the offerings had been left. Lifting the sleeping body of his new wife, he moved to the bath and stepped in, still cuddling her to his chest.

She awoke surrounded by gloriously warm water, feeling the gentle play of his hands on her back. He glanced down at her without moving and saw that she was awake, which promptly led him to take his hands from soothing to arousing.

He turned her so that she straddled his lap and caught her breasts in his hands, pushing one high and lowering his head to catch her nipple between his teeth. Swirling his tongue around it, then drawing it into his mouth and sucking on it hard, as her back bowed and arched.

Trailing one hand down her back he cupped one buttock in his hand and started to caress the tiny rosette of her anus.

Eiona whimpered and cried out, riding his hand greedily as a finger started to sneak through the tiny opening, her muscles working to accommodate him. Her pussy ached and wept with need and she shoved back against Kye desperately, crying out in shock when the movement buried two of his fingers inside her ass. The burning pain faded quickly, leaving her twisting on his hand, aching and hungry for more.

Kye released her nipple as the silken walls of her anus closed over his fingers—hot, tight and sweet. Surging from the bath, reveling in the strength he had in this new body, he carried her to the rug in front of the fire place again. With reluctance, he pulled his fingers from the tight clasp of her body and urged her to the floor, on her hands and knees.

He grabbed pillows and mounded them under her belly and found the little pot of sweet scented lubricant they had used the previous night. Putting it within easy reach, he dropped to his knees behind her and stared at her up-thrust ass, the tiny pink rosette, and lower to the naked, open lips and gleaming, red folds of her sex. He mounted her almost roughly, shoving the full length of his cock into her dripping passage, hot satisfaction rolling through him when she screamed and bore down around him in sudden, brutal climax.

As she came, he started to press and circle around her rosette, taking the lubricant and letting it dribble from the little clay pot to spill on the crevice between her butt cheeks, dripping down to coat her anus. Gathering it with his fingers, he started to probe the opening gently while he rode her through her orgasm and started coaxing another from her body.

When she started to move hungrily against him, he slid his thumb inside her ass, the muscles loosening just enough to allow him to ease inside. So tight, he thought, shuddering, trying to imagine how it would feel to drive his cock in there.

Eiona moaned raggedly, pushing back against him, seeking more. His cock. She wanted that long, lovely cock inside her backside. "Please, Kye," she whispered hotly. "More."

"We will," he promised. "Soon. Trust me," he urged her when she tried to argue and demand the *more* she had asked for right now. Reaching for her hand, he guided it underneath her, ordering her to play with her clit.

Eiona circled her fingers around her swollen throbbing clit, pinching the peaked flesh between her fingers, rubbing it hard and fast, then slower, as her body tightened, her pussy clenched, orgasm riding near. She hissed out a protest when Kye's cock pulled from her pussy, but then she felt him starting to probe the tiny opening to the most intimate passage in her body.

Kye reached for the pot of lubricant as he pulled out, pouring its contents into his palm and coating his shaft with it before stroking her quivering rosette, and beginning, again, to probe inside. With satisfaction, he noted that she was more relaxed there now.

And hungry.

She moved against his hands, lifting her ass and squirming as he worked more of the lubricant inside her ass. "This is going to hurt some, especially this first time," he warned her, grasping his cock and holding it steady as she started to nudge her anus against him.

"I want it," she whispered. "Please, Kye."

It did hurt her. She flinched and cried out as the burning pain threatened to tear her to pieces. She cried out and tried to pull away instinctively. "No," Kye said, digging his fingers into her hips and holding her still. "Push down. Just like you did when the dragon fucked you with the dildo."

"You're too big," she wailed. "It will not work."

"It will work. Just push down. The pain won't last long." Part of him wanted to back off. He had sodomized a number of women, and they had all loved it, especially Ashlyn, but it was a sexual act that took a lot of practice.

But the majority of his being insisted he do this. In a rough, arrogant voice, he said, "My priestess swore to do all in her power to make me happy. Remember?"

"Yes," she gasped out, still trying to squirm away.

"Then push down, damn it, and let me fuck your ass," he ordered, slapping her butt lightly. "I need it."

She stiffened in indignation, and Kye sensed the battle inside her. But she bore down on him with a wail and when her body opened that tiny bit, he pushed the head of his cock past the tight ring of muscles and growled in pleasure, sliding his hand around to fondle her dripping pussy and stroke her engorged clit.

There was a fine, minute trembling deep within her body, and a fever started to burn inside her as he pushed the thick ridge of his cock inside, pulling out, then pushing back in. She moaned with satisfaction, hot licks of liquid flame coursing through her as he pulled out the tiniest bit and worked his cock back inside, deeper this time. He repeated it until she had taken more than half of his cock and was crying out with pleasure.

He started rocking inside her, going no deeper, just slow, gentle rocks that drew his flesh tight and had him wanting to ram her hard and fast, while she screamed and cried out his name. The tiny stimulation there would move her closer to climax, but it wasn't enough to actually let her come.

When she started to move and rock back against him, the nerves inside him loosened and drained away as she started to enjoy it. She bucked and thrashed under him, pushing back and trying to take more than he would give her. His fingers, dripping with her juices, still played with her clit, and paused from time to time to pump inside her before pulling out.

He draped his body over her back, limiting how deeply he could take her while he purred into her ear, "Shall I stop?"

"Do not dare," she gasped, crying out as he plunged two fingers inside her vagina. His thumb circled over her clit as he did so, causing her internal walls to quiver around his invading flesh.

"Then you like this?" he asked, straightening and driving another inch into her tight sheath.

"By the ninth order, yes," she cried out, moving and trying to take more. "Kye, please. More," she whimpered, moving back against him.

He drove his shaft into her slowly, deeper and deeper with each stroke, until he was burying himself to the balls with each thrust. Staring down, he watched as her rosette stretched wide around him, felt the intense pleasure shoot from his cock outward, encompassing his whole body with every drive into that hot silken passage.

"Would you like to be double fucked?" he asked roughly. "Would that please you?"

"Yes. Yes, it would."

As if by magic, the door swung open and Eiona's head flew up, staring at the man standing there. Eagan. Kye smiled with satisfaction. "The dragon sent him here," he told her. "I called him, and he said he would find Eagan."

Eagan stared at them in shock and hunger. He had heard them before he entered of course, but he had assumed it would be more of the same, him tasting her delicious pussy, maybe getting to slide his cock inside her mouth again. His eyes trailed over their profiles and his cock began to throb.

Kye lifted her upright, wrapping his arms around her, holding her straight up, rocking just slightly inside her tight sheath. He threw a tight rein on his control as something inside her body clung to the head of his cock, trying to hold him greedily inside her. Lifting his head, he stared over her shoulder to Eagan. "Your priestess has need of you," he said gutturally.

His mouth dry, Eagan whispered softly, "What does my lady wish of me?"

Kye smiled, resting his chin on her shoulder. "Tell him what you wish, Eiona," he told her, emphasizing him with another, deeper rock of his hips.

She squirmed in his arms and cried out, one hand reaching for Eagan. She needed him inside her. The pleasure of having Kye in her bottom was still to near pain, but it was delicious and she loved it and she couldn't stop remembering the pictures she had gleaned from Kye's mind, the pleasure he and his friend had given to the red haired woman Ashlyn.

Reaching out, she said, "Fuck me. That is what I wish."

He shed his clothes so quickly, a number of lacings and threads broke and soon he was kneeling naked in front of her, staring at Kye over her shoulder. "I do not wish to hurt her," he said raggedly.

Eiona hissed, "Now, Eagan."

And though she wasn't his mistress, she was his lady, and his priestess and he had been raised to do all she would ever ask of him. Shoving the pillows aside, he swallowed, his mouth suddenly dry. "I've never done it like this before," he said, remembering the brief glimpse he had gotten of Kye as he lifted Eiona off his rod just slightly before letting her slide back down.

"Doesn't matter," Kye muttered. "She's tighter with me inside her, but she's wet, and it's the same pussy you fucked before."

Eagan started to push his cock into her and had to bite back a silent disagreement. No. This wasn't the same. She had never been so tight. Never been this wet before. He could feel the throbbing of Kye's cock through the thin wall of flesh between them as he slid into her tight, convulsing sheath.

He was panting by the time he could give her no more and she was crying out—screaming soft little screams—and moaning in little broken sounds. He pulled out, pushed back in, and shuddered wildly as he felt Kye's cock pass against his as the warrior pulled out. When Eagan started to retreat, Kye would push inside her.

Kye's senses were being flooded. The sharp scent of her lust filled the air, the sound of her madly pounding heart, the satin slicked walls of her ass clinging to him as he pulled out. With shifts of his body, shifts of hers, rough commands to

Eagan, he finally had them with Eagan underneath, thrusting upwards into her welcoming depths, while Eiona stayed on her hands and knees, allowing Kye full access to her ass. He started to ride her harder, pulling out and driving back in, feeling Eagan pick up speed as well, Kye's sac slapping against Eagan's as they fucked her mercilessly.

Eiona screamed, then bucked as Kye slapped her ass hard. The burning pain from that flared hot and bright inside, shoving her a little closer to the edge. Another pounding thrust from Kye shoved her completely over and she fell screaming into climax, the hot burning waves washing over her, scalding her, stealing her breath.

She wanted to fall into oblivion, but Kye said something to Eagan over her shoulder and she felt a hot mouth close over the point of one nipple. Above her, Kye shoved her hips lower, and filled her with deep, driving digs of his cock, Eagan pounding into her pussy forcefully. Their hungers fed hers, and she felt the need break open inside her again.

"That's it, sweetie," Kye was murmuring against her ear as he coaxed her into taking more. He was able to completely bury his cock inside her ass now, and she gloried in it, taking the delicious painful pleasure and screaming with it.

Kye felt it inside her body, felt as she gave way totally and completely to him. Gripping her hips with his hands, he started to ream her ass hard and rough, growling when she tried to move underneath. She stilled and fell heavily onto Egan's chest, submitting to Kye's needs.

Eagan pushed up into her, staring at her glowing, sexy face, reveling in the tight, wet clasp of her creamy sheath. Each thrust from Kye rippled through Eagan and he gritted his teeth, resisting the urge to flood her body. His testicles ached and throbbed as each thrust had Kye's sac briefly caressing his. His rod was swollen and aching and hot inside the wet embrace of her cleft. He pushed upward as he felt Kye retreat, his muscled body shuddering when Kye forced her down, causing her to take Eagan higher and deeper, bringing her clit into contact with his body.

She screamed and tightened around them, her entire body arching and contracting as she came, starting with slow shudders that increased in strength and duration, both of her invaded portals tightening and clenching around the penetrating cocks until both men bellowed and filled her with seed, her body milking it from them hungrily.

Eiona collapsed against Egan, black dots swirling and looming larger and larger in her vision, before she finally gave up and tumbled into unconscious oblivion.

Kye felt it when her body went slack but he held still, letting the raging orgasm finish with him as he pumped the last of his seed into her ass. Only then, did he pull out, taking her with him, pulling her off of Eagan and curling her into the embrace of his body.

"Is she well?" Egan asked, his chest heaving, his cock wet and slick with her juices and his own climax. And his eyes were worried.

"She passed out," Kye murmured, exhaustion crowding his mind. "She'll be fine."

Egan started to push up but his muscles felt like jelly. And the amused knowledge in the warrior's slumberous eyes told him that the other man knew how he felt. "Get some rest, kid," Kye murmured, burying his face in her hair, snagging a blanket from the side and throwing it over their three bodies. "Such pleasure will nearly kill you."

Eagan gave up the fight to rise and leave them to their privacy. After all, the dragon had told him Kye wished him to come. He had been summoned. They'd tell him when they were done, right?

* * * * *

Something was wrong.

Of course, that wasn't hard to figure out because Kye's first clue was a sharp, short scream that came from Eiona, startling him into wakefulness. Her eyes were wide open and blank, and if Kye hadn't heard the faint sound of her heart, slowing down even as he stared at her face, he would have thought she was dead.

Eagan still lay on his side, eyes closed as if in sleep. But he wasn't sleeping. Not dead, not asleep, but not awake either. Frozen.

Kye reached out, trying to find that path he used to speak with the dragon, but it was blocked, seemingly barricaded by snow and ice and pain.

He rose slowly, the fine hair on his nude body raised and prickled. Cocking his head, he listened. Silence. Not just inside the lodge, but without. And it shouldn't be quiet. If he guessed right, it was well into the day, and a breakfast buffet lay cold on the table.

An odd blue glow caught his eye and he turned his head and stared at his sword. *Aldrian-elai* lay glowing, pulsing and throbbing. Oddly enough, each time the sword's light pulsed, so did Kye's heart. Whispers of old knowledge, the old body's memories rushed through his head.

Magic.

Whatever froze the people was some sort of magic. And *Aldrian-elai* protected Kye. Eiona should have been protected, simply by dint of what she was. But something had attacked the dragon as well, and when it wounded him, it had ripped through Eiona like a poisoned dagger.

Kye grabbed his pants and jerked them on, ignoring the rest of his clothes, taking the naked, glowing blade in his hand. "Fallen into some kind of Tolkien nightmare," he muttered, reminded of the movie, where Frodo had drawn his blue blade, Sting as Orcs swarmed all around them, right as Aragorn told him to run. "Problem is...they really were warriors."

131

And Kye still didn't feel like one.

A sigh seemed to fill the room, and Kye felt a prodding in his mind. *Warrior.*

He narrowed his eyes and stared at the sword.

Warrior.

"Holy shit, now the fucking sword is talking to me," he griped, wanting to release the blade, unwilling to do so.

You are warrior. Let me show —

A barrier inside his mind fell and Kye felt a strangled scream die in his throat as his soul completely merged with the knowledge Rue had possessed, and felt the essence that filled the sword swell inside him. He fell to his knees, his throat locked around that scream, as images of battle and blood stained his mind.

The sword. It was the link between the warrior Rue had been trained as, and Kye. When he rose, his feet were steady and his mind full. New knowledge rested there and Kye shifted his grip on the sword's pommel and strode from the tent.

He moved silently through the streets, staring in dismay at the people frozen around him. It was like time had stopped.

What is doing this?

The sword pulsed once, brightly, more harshly than the norm, then an almost gentle play of light and the answer was suddenly just there.

A man, the one who had paid for Eiona's kidnapping.

A mage, someone born with true magic, and an evil one.

He held sway over them with mind magic and the sword suspected he had poisoned Eilrah. That was the only thing that would account for why Eilrah wasn't there, why Kye couldn't reach him, and why Eiona had screamed a death scream and lay frozen. Kye didn't want to think about it, but he suspected she hovered near death.

132

"She dies," he said flatly, knowing somebody listened. "You die." Then he laughed. "Well, that's not fair. You're gonna die anyway. But if she dies, you're gonna die...slow." He drew it out as he neared the village square, turning in a slow circle.

He felt the hot lash of anger, malice, and dismay.

Why wasn't I frozen?

Again, the sword pulsed brightly. And he knew. The sword was protecting him, the way it would only protect the *elai*. And whoever had done this hadn't been prepared for Kye's freedom. Rue may have been born into the body, but the sword hadn't bonded with him the way it would bond with a true warrior. Their attacker hadn't been prepared for Kye to be able to fight.

"Surprise," Kye growled, whirling and facing the lunging attack. He felt one brief moment of shock as he saw a face he recognized. The village wise man. But then he whirled his arm over head and struck out, clashing with the wicked metal blade that gleamed wetly.

A harsh, peculiar scent stung the air. *Dragon's bane,* the sword whispered. *The blade is poisoned.*

Sparks flew as the two swords met. Kye grinned tauntingly into the wise man's face before shoving out, causing the smaller man to falter and stumble. He wanted to know only one thing—if Eiona's magic was the ability to see inside the soul, how come she hadn't seen this one?

Why hadn't that rather spectacular little girl seen?

The wise man lunged again, an odd, almost hesitant lunge, as if he had changed his mind about attacking, and then about not attacking. Kye moved gracefully out of reach, and later he would be shocked by the ease of the movement, the way his body moved as if he had been born just to fight this fight.

He felt a brief throb from the blade, something that felt like surprise, and then satisfaction, as if it had figured out a rather tricky riddle. *Two souls, one body. Something else holds sway over him and it has been inside him since birth. Two minds trapped inside one body, two souls.*

And now he was facing a psycho with a spilt personality. Kye fought the urge to groan in frustration and snapped out silently, *Be quiet. Let me fight.* He'd deal with the puzzles and the whys and what-for's later. He snaked back as the tip of the deadly sword parted the soft leather on his thigh, leaving the skin unmarked.

The glee in the attacker's eyes faded as Kye taunted, "Better luck next time." Then his blade moved in a whirl of silver-blue, hacking, slicing, stabbing. And disarming. The deadly blade flew away and time seemed to slow as Kye pivoted, whirled, *Aldrian-elai* lifted high for a death strike.

He must die, warrior. The hold he has over the village will not end unless he willingly ends it. Or dies.

Kye stared into the wise man's face and saw it there. He wouldn't relinquish his hold. He'd rather die. With a snarl, Kye said, "Glad to oblige," as he swung *Aldrian-elai* in a sweeping arc, severing the man's head from his shoulders.

All around him, life resumed. But not as if time had simply restarted. They had been aware, and watching everything.

Screams erupted and panicked, babbling people rushed him but Kye turned and ran. The handmaidens. If anybody would know how to combat poison, they should. He found the handmaidens at Eiona's side and wanted to scream with frustration. They only stared at him with tearful, helpless eyes as Eiona lay still, caught and frozen.

Forever, if they didn't find Eilrah and purge the poison from his system.

He heard a soft, young voice and lifted his head, watched as Rianne slid through the door of the lodge. All of nine, and far too much world-weary knowledge in her young eyes. Kye realized with a start that this was what people meant when they said a person had an old soul. Behind stood the youngest wise man, his face wet with tears—sorrow, grief and anger lining his face—making him seem twenty years older.

"Come," she ordered, holding out her tiny hand to Kye. "I can help you."

All around, voices panicked and shrieked and babbled. Just a child, a child. They needed true magic. Their priestess was dying.

"Enough," Kye hissed. And then louder, "Enough."

The wise man ignored them and beckoned for Kye. "I know where to find what we need. Rianne already knows how to use it. But we must hurry."

It was nightfall before the antidote was ready. It was in two forms, one a paste to coat the wound and seal it, keeping any of the poison that still coated his scales from seeping in. The other was a thick, noxious liquid which Kye had the pleasure of administering.

Eagan and the wise man held the dragon's massive head up, while Kye forced his jaws open and poured the antidote in. Once it was done, he fell to the ground, stroking the sharp spines that rose from Eilrah's head. "Bring Eiona," he said to Eagan. "Hurry."

It seemed hours passed, but it was only moments before the lad was striding back into the clearing where they had found Eilrah's body, carrying Eiona, her eyes still open and staring, her breathing growing more shallow as each second passed.

Eagan laid her in Kye's lap, tucking a blanket he had thrown over his shoulder around her cold body.

Then he retreated to join Rianne and the wise man Sol where they waited near the trees. Hours passed.

Kye rocked Eiona, humming softly under his breath, stroking her back. Was she warmer?

A rough smoke filled breath filled the clearing and Kye's eyes widened as Eiona and Eilrah both gasped simultaneously. The dragon jerked up and away before he started to vomit and Eiona spilled from Kye's lap to do the same as they purged their bodies. Eiona hadn't been poisoned, but she was linked to Eilrah closely. In time, their hearts would even beat as one. And what afflicted one, afflicted the other.

Kye wrapped his body around hers as she shuddered and emptied her stomach.

Rianne came closer, smiling down at Kye, her young face glowing and happy. "She will be fine," the child promised. "Both of them will be."

"I know," Kye said, his voice thick with tears of relief. "Thank you, my little lady."

She smiled and darted off into the woods, the wolven at her heels, laughing like the child she was.

* * * * *

Kye curled around Eiona's shaking body later that night, his cock stiff and aching against her naked butt. He made no move to mount her though. Her mind and soul were fine, but her body would be sick for some time.

"I love you," he whispered into her hair, the need for her clawing through his gut.

He felt her shock and then he gasped as they tumbled free from their bodies, into the rainbow of shifting colors and lights that was the spirit land. "Show me," Eiona begged, pulling his body to hers. She spread her thighs and Kye shuddered as the rainbow played over the naked lips of her sex, her wet, exposed folds.

"You're sick," he groaned as her hands closed eagerly over his cock and tried to guide him inside her.

"Not here. Here I am whatever I want to be. And I want to be mating," she told him.

136

He let her guide him inside her before he brushed her hands away. Propping his weight on his elbows, he drove his hips hard and sent his aching cock into the very heart of her, feeling the mouth of her womb open slightly around him, greedily, like even that part of her ached for him.

He shifted so that he stroked the hard little bud of her clit with every thrust, moving until he was riding her high on her body, fucking her wet warm embrace hungrily. He caught the cheek of her ass in his hand, brought her thighs up to his hip, digging his fingers into the warm crevice of her bottom, and she shrieked with pleasure, tightening around him.

Kye stared into her eyes, feeling the sharp aching need for her, the love that made his heart ache every time he looked at her. "I love you," he whispered against her mouth before moving to kiss the tears away from her cheeks.

"I love you," she cried out, holding him tightly to her, reveling in the deep thrusts of his cock that stole her breath, clenching her muscles around his cock as he buried himself inside her. She loved him, this man she had waited for. It had taken an age, it seemed, to find him and she wouldn't let him go, ever. "Harder, fuck me harder, Kye. Mark me."

He shuddered as she whispered in his ear and he drove harder into her wet sheath, crying out when she convulsed around him. He pulled out, until the head of his thick cock rested between her wet pouting lips and then he burrowed back in, sinking into the wet clutch of her pussy and shaking with the pleasure of it.

He wanted to ride her forever, but his need overcame his want and he exploded into her as she bore down on him, her sweet little body tightening and convulsing around him, milking the seed from his cock, slowly, lingering, until they fell against each other, the lights playing around them.

* * * * *

Kye woke up in the lodge, feeling the warm weight of her body as she slept against him.

For some reason, Ashlyn sprung into his mind, their wedding, their honeymoon, odd little bits of their life together.

And then Eiona, standing naked in the open air, arms out as she called Eilrah. Eiona shuddering and shaking as the dragon used his magic to bring her to orgasm as he helped initiate her ass. Their bonding.

And the moment when Eilrah had looked at him after the dragon and priestess had purged their bodies. When those odd red-gold eyes looked into his and the dragon rasped out, "Thank you."

What a lucky bastard he had turned out to be, he mused.

In the span of one life-time, he was getting to live two lives. And had been allowed to love two very special women.

And of course, he thought mockingly, feeling the distant stroke of Eilrah's mind on his, he had gotten a smart assed dragon to boot.

The End.

DRAGON'S WOMAN

ഌ

Chapter One

ઇઝ

Rianne stood at the outskirts of the village, one hand curled around her staff, the other indolently tapping her thigh.

What she wanted to do was hide. Wrap her arms around herself and retreat.

She'd come to the village to buy a few of the necessities that she couldn't raise or make herself in the solitude of the forest and as always, she felt like a pariah.

Egan, bless his heart, had agreed to bring her purchases to her, but he hadn't been alone. The man at his side was one she only vaguely remembered from childhood, but he kept staring at her as though he expected her to turn him to stone.

Part of her had wanted to make a nasty face at him, just to see if he'd jump. The other part... Closing her eyes, she turned away from the village, stared into the dark heart of the woods and wished she could undo time.

They feared her.

They all feared her.

Even her teachers had feared her after what had happened.

But Rianne didn't know what else she could have done. She'd been at the school for nearly four years when the attack came. She'd been sleeping outside—that was something she did often—in the silence of the gardens. By the time the screams had woken her, it had been too late.

All of her teachers, the first ones, the ones who had understood her, loved her, had died first. Many of the students had been killed as well. Only the first year trainees were spared and that was because they had still been young enough to be molded.

The men who had come in the dead of the night were mages, trained in the paths of blood, caring for little beyond furthering their power.

Twenty of them.

She had come on them as they were carrying the unconscious first year students from the keep. They were surrounded by the bodies of the women who had rushed to protect the school.

Her clearest memory was of Taya. The sweet old lady had taught herb magicks and Rianne had adored her. She had been killed, gutted from the looks of it, by something not human. And tossed aside like she was nothing.

It was that sight that had made her snap.

The carnage the mages had left behind was nothing compared to what Rianne had done. She hadn't any idea what she was doing, just knew that she had wanted *them* to suffer as they had made these women and girls suffer.

And suffer they had.

But sadly, so had the first year students. The spells used to hold them in sleep had shattered as Rianne attacked. They had stood, screaming in terror as Rianne killed twenty men without so much as moving a muscle. There hadn't been enough left of the men to even try piecing them together.

The lands were splattered with gore, blood and tissue—as were the girls.

Three of the nine had been ruined. The emotional trauma had run so deep, their magick splintered. Priestesses who came from miles away had been forced to silence the magick before it fully bloomed, leaving the girls little more than empty shells of what they had been.

The other six were fostered out separately—Rianne never saw any of them again.

And she had been sent to a school in the far south, away from all she had known and loved. Ten years there. A witch's schooling usually ended when she reached eighteen, or after she'd been through seven years of training. She should have schooled for only three more years, but instead, they had taken another seven years of her life.

To master that wild magick—"We must never ever see that dark display of power again."

Those words had been spoken to her so many times, she could hear them in her sleep.

When she had finally been deemed safe, she'd been twenty-one. She'd returned north, desperate to be once more among those who loved and welcomed her. But instead, they all feared her.

Tales of the slaughter at Miden School had spread across the land and all who saw her remembered nothing more than those three young girls. Three young girls Rianne had nearly pushed into madness.

It would have been better if she had never woke that night—or if she had been killed along with her companions and teachers. They hadn't seen her actions as anything more than a bloodbath by some wild, unknown savage.

Only a handful of the people in her village could look at her without fear in their eyes.

Part of her wished there was someplace else she could go, but she had been called back home, and home she would stay.

The sound of footsteps approaching pulled her from the miserable well of her thoughts and she opened her eyes, forcing a smile for Egan.

The man in his wake, she ignored as best she could.

Should have been easy—she had been dealing with fear and distaste for too many years of her life.

Should have been...

* * * * *

Eiona smiled at Kye as he moved into the lodge, but her smile faded as she saw the dark scowl on his face.

"What is wrong?" she murmured, stepping up to him and wrapping her arms around his waist.

"I spoke with Egan."

He fell silent and Eiona sighed. There were times that getting water from stone would be easier than making him speak.

"How is he?"

He looked up, his eyes sparking with fury. "Madder than hell. Just like me. Rianne still will not come into the village."

Eiona sighed. "The villagers fear her, lover. She feels that. Being here would likely make her ill."

"They shouldn't be afraid," he snarled, whirling away and starting to pace, circling around the lodge with long angry strides. "She isn't the bad guy."

"No. She is not. But she did something no witch should be able to do. Something none of us should be able to do. She has a wild power—it is stronger than anything many of us have ever seen. It makes her different. People have always feared anything different."

Eiona decided it was best to not tell Kye that she could understand the villager's feelings. Rianne was...dangerous.

Kye stopped by the fireplace and hunkered down on his heels in front of it. As he stared into the flames, he whispered, "She was a child. Terrified and traumatized. All she did was kill those who would have killed her if they could have. How much longer should she have to suffer for that? She did nothing wrong."

Eiona moved up behind him and wrapped her arms around him. One big warm hand came up, closing around her wrist. "No, she did not. But we both know that it rarely is that simple."

144

"There's nothing we can do, is there?" Kye asked quietly.

Pressing a kiss to his neck, she whispered, "I do not know."

He moved then, up and around, so fast that she fell back away from him and onto her rump, off balance. He moved between her splayed thighs, cupping her face in his hands. "I love you, wife."

Eiona smiled up at him. "And I love you, husband."

As he covered her mouth with his, Eiona wrapped her arms around his neck and arched against him. She wanted nothing more than to erase that sadness from his eyes.

Falling to her back, she held up her arms and whispered, "Come to me, husband. Make love to me."

* * * * *

Sunning himself in the field, Eilrah lifted his face to the sky and stretched, feeling the muscles inside his powerful body unfurl, the tension of the past weeks slowly draining away.

Well, some of it. Not all. All of it would not leave until he gave in to the urge to find himself a female and mate. A thick plume of smoke drifted from his nares and a rumble rose from deep in his chest. Sexual need spread through him — taut, palpable, heavy. He ached, he hungered, something he hadn't truly experienced until he had bonded with his priestess.

Not in any of the forms he wore.

Never, never had he realized what would happen when he bonded so deeply with Eiona and Kye all those years ago. Granted, he was a young dragon, and had not taken a priestess bond before. You would *think* one of the elders would have shared such knowledge with him.

It certainly would have made his life a bit easier over the past few years if he had known what to expect. The first time, he hadn't fought it, even though he hadn't known what was

145

happening. It was magick—magick was a part of him and he had always accepted it.

But when the magick cleared and he could see through the glittering red smoke that had wrapped around him, he was much, *much* closer to the ground than he had ever been. From a height of nearly fifty feet to not even six. The scales of ruby red were gone and instead, he had worn smooth, human skin.

And he had *ached*.

For a while, he had fought the urge to change, but when he did it brought pain—physical pain. Eventually, he had stopped fighting and followed his instincts.

It had been instinct that had brought him to this clearing in the forest this morning, instead of flying farther away.

As he stretched out, he caught a scent.

The rich scent of woman drifted to him and Eilrah lifted his head, tantalized.

Hmmm…tasty. Rich, spicy, young.

Familiar, powerful. Eilrah was drawn, entirely too drawn, and too damn hungry to continue ignoring such a fine, ripe scent. Stretching out with his mind, he made sure none were in the forest around them…and released the other inside him.

Ripples of magick burst through the clearing, and inside him it was thick, hot and potent. A fine red mist rose just above his scales and they started to shimmer and dissolve. His form shrank and condensed as heat raced along his skin, through him, and he threw his head back, trumpeting to the sky.

* * * * *

It had been nearly a week since her latest trip to the village and the depression that had been settling around her only deepened.

Even moving through the forest, letting the life and power ebb around her did little to soothe her mind.

146

When the deep, piercing cry shattered the silence, she almost welcomed it. She knew the sound—Eiona's dragon. Eilrah, the great red dragon, calling out, singing that wild dragon's cry. Isha lifted his head under her palm, a soft lupine whimper escaping his throat as he looked up at her. She smiled down at him. "The dragon sounds lonely, doesn't he?" the young witch asked softly.

She understood loneliness.

Since she had returned home, Rianne had learned to understand loneliness very well. Just one year. She had been home a year. Yet she had never been more alone.

At first, a few friends from her childhood had come deep into the heart of the forest to see her, but they had seen the stark, unsmiling woman she had become and eventually, they'd left, never to return.

Perhaps seeing the silent shadow she now was only reinforced all of the stories they had heard about her. Or maybe they had looked at her and seen the same thing she saw.

Death and pain.

She didn't know. But no one came now.

She saw Egan on rare trips close to the village, and from time to time, Kye happened upon her in the forest, but other than that…she was alone.

In her heart, she wondered why she had come at all. These people did not need her. Eiona served them well and good. But when Rianne had searched her soul for where she must set up her keep, when she had prayed to the Sacrificed God, she was given the answer in her dreams. She must return home.

So home Rianne had come. She had made her home deep in the woods—away from the village, away from the reminders of a life she wouldn't ever have.

Seeing the happiness in the village made her yearn for her own.

So yes, she understood loneliness.

Drawn to the long, trumpeting call, she rose, the beaded fringe on her belt swaying around her hips as she strode through the woods. Isha followed, his tongue lolling out of his mouth as he trotted easily at her side. *Not going to find the dragon there. His other self*, the wolven said abruptly, pausing to scent the air.

"Eiona?" Rianne asked curiously. She could smell the dragon's sulfur and musk as she ducked around a tree, her fingers wrapped loosely around her staff. At the end of the staff, a wide jagged piece of roughly hewn sapphire sat, glowing deep within. It pulsed, in echo to her heartbeat.

No…not the priestess. The dragon's other self. His skin. The one who walks on two legs.

Rianne was perplexed.

She expected, perhaps, to find Kye.

Instead, she entered an empty clearing.

Her sharp nose caught the scent of a male. That scent was warm, musky—entirely too appealing. So appealing, it was damn near too late when she scented the sulfuric, sour scent of *Saphicate*.

Saphicates—the two legged, intelligent creatures that had begun to haunt their woods. Whirling, she stumbled back and fell, dodging the swiping claws just in time to miss having them take her throat out.

* * * * *

Eilrah had scented the young witch just before he'd scented the small band of *Saphicates*. In mortal form, he was less dangerous…but just a little. A feral grin revealed wickedly sharp teeth as he reached overhead, pulling himself into the tree just at the edge of the clearing. Muscles bulged, tawny golden skin flashed as he disappeared into the leaves, a soft whisper of illusion hiding the mark of his passing. *Saphicates* entered the clearing and hid themselves only moments before the young witch emerged from the concealing cover of trees, her soft blue eyes narrowed and watchful.

Her thick black hair was woven into a fat braid that hung down to her knees. She held her witch's staff in her left hand, her right flexed and ready. Already, she knew something was amiss. A warrior witch, not a healer, this one.

There was something familiar about her. Eilrah's topaz eyes, shot through with glints of red, narrowed as she started to turn, her eyes watchful. The first *Saphicate* lunged at her from out of the thicket and Eilrah growled, but she had already dropped and rolled, hissing under her breath and striking out with her staff. Blue flame shot out and struck the green-skinned humanoid in the chest and it fell back shrieking as its companions swarmed out of the trees.

Eilrah dropped down out of a tree and flashed them an evil grin, snarling threateningly as four of them advanced toward the fallen witch, thinking she'd be an easy target. The young witch had already flipped onto her feet, though, laughing tauntingly as she struck the earth with the butt of her staff, sending more blue flame flaring across the earth in a straight line for the *Saphicates* who shrieked and bellowed, snarling at her in their hissing, high-pitched tongue, backing away warily from the deadly flame.

Three more launched out of hiding and lunged for Eilrah. Catching the first one by the neck, he opened his mouth and roared, fire falling from his lips, heat rising from his hand, as he burned it to ash. He caught the scent of the witch's blood, ripe with adrenaline, her heartbeat pounding fast and furious as he launched himself at the other two, slashing out with the nails of one hand to rip out the throat of one, crushing it, burning it with his dragon's fiery touch as he turned to face his third and final foe.

The witch was facing her opponents across a line of blue flame, a cocky grin on her face as Eilrah wiped the blood from his hands, grimacing in distaste at the foul stench of it. She cast him one brief, unreadable glance before looking at the remaining *Saphicates* and, in a low, steady voice, emulating their hissing language, she said, "Dead lay your companions, by strength or magick. Do you wish to follow?"

Eilrah had to use mind magick to hear their reply as they said, "You will die, witch. We came for your blood. We will leave with it."

She smiled sweetly. "Glad to oblige." Her staff hovered in midair as she drew a blade and pricked her finger as Eilrah hesitated, disturbed by the glint in her eyes, and that sweet smile. Blood welled from her finger and a fat, rosy drop plopped to the ground, and the *Saphicates* started to realize just how much trouble they were in.

The earth trembled and shook, and a great rumbling shriek tore a rent in the ground and smoke filled the air around the *Saphicates*, leaving Eilrah blind.

By the time it was over, the *Saphicates* were left waist deep in the earth, stone cold. And dead. Eilrah barely had time to clear the smoke from his eyes before she had turned on him, her staff crossed defensively in front of her.

"Be at ease, little witch." Lifting his hands calmingly, he smiled a charming, crooked grin. "I mean no harm, none a 'tall."

The staff didn't lower. "I trust no warrior with such strange, powerful magick. Burning a creature with merely your touch? What are you doing here? Where did you come from?"

Eilrah felt the subtle touch of "truth seek" falling into the earth around his feet as she spoke, a touch few would have felt. If he hadn't been a creature born of the elements, he would not have. But a great red dragon, a creature of fire, would always feel anything that touched the elements. As would a witch…peering at her, he studied those soft blue eyes and felt recognition sing through his veins.

He hadn't seen her since she was a child.

But this was no child before him now.

Rianne...the young witch who had befriended Kye all those years ago. A powerful one, a wise one, even for one so young.

"I have dwelt in these parts for many years," he said obliquely, lifting his face to the sun and closing his eyes. "I came out to feel the sun, to rest, to relax. And I scented the *Saphicates* only a moment after I scented you, young witch."

And only a few moments before I planned on seducing you. He wisely kept that thought to himself. Eilrah still had every intention of feeling the young witch beneath him soon. Even knowing who she was wouldn't change his plans.

She studied him with narrowed eyes. One corner of his mouth lifted in a small smile as he lowered his face and opened his eyes, a thick lock of black hair falling onto his forehead as he met her sapphire gaze.

"You're not from the village."

"No, I am not," he responded agreeably. "I care nothing for village life." Not to mention it was far too confining for a dragon's mass. And the fact that he could take a mortal's form had just never come up with his priestess. As time passed, he had to take mortal form more often, every few days, and if he lived in the village, somebody would know. A brief frown darkened his face and his eyes glowed more red than golden, sending a gasp through Rianne that he did not notice. What would Eiona say? 'Twas really quite a puzzle.

Inhaling, he drank in Rianne's warm, womanly scent, fixing his gaze first on her naked feet, planted so confidently on the forest floor. Eilrah imagined she walked barefoot nigh everywhere, until it grew too cold for her to tolerate it. A skintight suit clung to her, supple, grass green, leaving her arms bare, veeing down between her breasts, fastening with small ties that ran from between her breasts to her navel. Around her waist, she wore a beaded, fringed belt, decorated with shades of blue and green, the beads clacking and swaying with her every move. Random pouches hung here and there, and she had returned the blade to the belt at her left hip.

She looked wild and enchanting, he decided. She had been enchanting as a child, sweet and precocious—innocent.

Looking into her sad, watchful eyes, he wondered what had taken the innocence away, and he decided if he could find it, he would burn it into oblivion.

"You grew into quite the lovely thing, Rianne," Eilrah said with a wolfish smile. And then he darted into the woods, his own naked feet swift and silent.

* * * * *

Those haunting, amazing eyes had been disturbingly familiar.

Topaz, golden, shot through with streaks the color of rubies.

And he knew her.

Not just her name. Something about the way he looked at her made her think he had known her from before, as a child, when she had still been training. Shaking her head, Rianne whispered, "You are becoming fanciful, like the daydreaming first year students back at the school. You've no idea where your destiny lies, but it seems to be nothing of pleasantness."

With a morose sigh, she turned back to the chore at hand. How considerate of her unknown comrade to leave her with the task of burning the bodies. All around knew that to leave a dead *Saphicate* was to ask for more of their numbers to come searching for vengeance.

"Might I be of assistance?"

That deep rumbling voice—arrogant and self-possessed— boomed out from behind her as the great red dragon snaked out from the trees in his smaller form. He had two, the one he wore now, and the larger dragon form that seemed to blot out the sky when he rose on his hindquarters.

Now, as he rose up and studied the *Saphicates*, his triangular head was only three times higher than the witch's.

Instead of six. His red and gold scales winked at her in the sun as Eilrah lowered himself to the ground, turning to study her, blinking thickly lashed eyes slowly, breathing and blowing out a puff of smoke as he cocked his head.

"Shall I take care of this little…mess, lady witch?"

"I'm fully capable of burning bodies, Red Dragon," Rianne said coolly. Presenting him with her back, she lifted one arm and pointed her staff at the three *Saphicates* that were buried and frozen in the ground. As their bodies began to burn, a foul stench flooded the air.

"Capable, aye. Very capable," Eilrah replied soberly, his eyes flashing with mirth as she turned back, her own eyes filling with tears as the stench robbed her of her breath. "And does their stink please you? I had sought to save you from it."

She was nearly gagging on her own bile as the stench of it filled her head. Eilrah moved closer and his bulk forced her back against a tree, the scent of dragon musk and sulfur filling her head, chasing back the stink of burning *Saphicate*.

"It worsens if they haven't been dead long, witch," he murmured. Keeping his bulk and the rather pleasant scent of his body between them, he turned, and Rianne shrieked, startled as heat surrounded and nearly burned her as he blasted the *Saphicates*.

Eilrah didn't burn them. He incinerated them…to ashes.

But nary a bade of grass was burned, and not a single leaf was scorched.

The only scent in the air now was the fading scent of dragon fire, pungent and ripe, but sweet. And dragon musk.

The great red dragon backed away, smiling with his mouth gaping open as he studied her pale face.

"Mortals, you and your damn pride." He turned and launched himself into the air, his black wings beating the sky as Rianne struggled to catch her breath.

Chapter Two

🔊

A flash of gold through the trees a few days later had her heart racing.

When Rianne caught the odd, unique scent of his skin on the breeze, her mouth went dry.

It was him. Whoever he was.

Sliding around the rocks that encircled the little-known bathing pools, she studied him as he dove into the deepest end of the pool, swimming over to the shallow edges where the falls tumbled down in a natural shower.

As he rose, the water sluiced down his golden skin, slicking his black hair back from his face in a smooth cap, leaving the chiseled bones of his face stark and unframed.

"Did you come for a swim?"

Rianne smiled, lowering herself to the grassy knoll. She should have known that he would know she was there. "No. 'Tis too cool for me. I am just walking the woods. Do you not feel the cold?"

When he turned to face her, Rianne felt liquid lightning race through her and pool in her loins. His eyes were swirling and sparking, and his body was long and lean. And hungry. The thick heavy length of his cock was hard, jutting upright as he moved slowly in her direction. Small puffs of steam rose from his body as he moved, and when he knelt at her side, Rianne felt that heat. "Ahh…no, I guess you don't feel the cold. What are you doing?"

A slow, heated smile tugged at his mouth and he replied, "Talking?" As he spoke, so close to her, she noticed something she hadn't before. His tongue…it was oddly shaped, more pointed, almost like that of a serpent, although it lacked that forked quality. His teeth were wickedly sharp and pointed.

He wasn't human.

Forcing her thoughts back to his response, she asked sardonically, "In the nude?"

"I came here wearing this skin." He shrugged. "I brought no clothes." He reached over, and tugged the scarf from her shoulder, flipping it over his lap. "Since it bothers you, I can…"

A slow shaky breath left her lips. Something about the thought of her things covering him, touching his naked body, made her body go soft and weak inside. "Suit yourself," she responded easily, thankful she was able to keep her voice level. "Do you have a name?"

"Rah."

Rianne felt her breath catch as he slid one hand through her thick inky hair. "Lovely, lovely witch," he murmured. "You suffered no ill effects from your encounter with the *Saphicates*?"

"No. Witches are immune to the poisons they pass." A *Saphicate* could pass a magickal poison through the air they breathed out—one of the reasons they were so deadly. It went into the bloodstream and slowed a person's reflexes, could even stop them, leaving them easy prey. "It's rather obvious all your faculties are in order, too."

Rah smiled, a slow, sexy curl of his chiseled mouth that had her blood simmering just below a boil. "Aye. My…faculties are in order. Such a pretty thing you became, Rianne," he said, reaching up and tracing his finger down her cheek. "So soft, so strong."

Her breath came sliding out of her in a shuddering sigh and she had to swallow the knot in her throat before she could speak. "How do you know me? Why don't I remember you?"

Those amazing, jewel-like eyes gleamed. "You were a young child when you left," he offered, cocking a brow. But she knew, as did he, that wasn't the reason.

Slowly she narrowed her eyes, studying him closely. Those eyes, that amazing scent, the pointed tongue, his teeth, the heat that rolled from his body like…

Rah…

He was waiting.

Waiting to see if she could remember. "You wear another form besides this mortal one, do you not?" she asked carefully.

Those eyes… But how could it be?

"Indeed I do. This one, in fact, takes over more often than I care for it to. The mortal form has needs, desires…hungers…that I cannot ignore now that I have spent so much time wearing this skin," he said. "But what other form, do you know?"

"There are so few people here who are able to wander through these woods, live in them, without setting my nerves afire. It would have to be another elemental magicker. And you are not a stranger to these parts, I do not think," Rianne said slowly. *You are mad, witch, to even think it.*

"I am an elemental," he conceded.

"Not an elemental…*the* elemental. This land here is your charge, as it is to the priestess Eiona. Your priestess," Rianne said as it became too impossible to ignore the rich golden red of his eyes, and the tantalizing scent that rose from his body. "But how does a great red dragon walk on two legs? In mortal skin?"

"I knew you were a quick one," he said, grinning. "A great red dragon who bonded too deeply with his priestess mate. I took too much of her essence inside myself and this mortal coil is one I must take every few days. When I bonded with Eiona, our souls and heart merged—too much of her humanity spilled into me."

"So it makes you human?" she asked doubtfully, arching a brow.

"No. Nothing can make me human," he said patiently. "I am dragon. But no longer completely dragon. I walk between the two worlds now. It's terribly discomfiting at times." Under his lashes, he studied her closely and Rianne felt her face heat and knew she shouldn't ask, but she couldn't stop herself.

"Discomfiting, huh?"

A wolfish smile spread across his face and Rianne felt heat pool in her belly as he shifted, moving so that he had one knee on each side of her thigh, his thighs cradling hers. "I hunger...I ache...I feel the needs she spilled inside me during our bonding, yet so very rarely can I indulge," he whispered, cupping her cheek in one hand. "It rides me, the need to feel a woman against me, beneath me, to hear her moans, her cries...her screams as she comes around me. Aye, discomfiting."

Her heart started to gallop in her chest as he leaned forward, threading both hands through her hair and lowering his face to nuzzle her neck. "Sweet, soft woman, powerful, wild witch—the scent of you is intoxicating." His voice had dropped to a gruff, rumbling purr that reverberated in his chest as he moved so that he was straddling her lap, pinning her in place. "I've a yen to have a taste. No...the whole feast."

His heat seemed to reach across the scant distance separating them, heating her skin until Rianne felt a light sweat break out over her body. Rianne felt the cream flood her cleft and her nipples hardened to near pain at his words.

His hands trailed over her body and she gasped as he shifted and took her mouth with his. He drove his tongue deep inside her mouth as his hand cupped the back of her neck. His tongue...so incredibly agile, and rougher than a human male, dancing in her mouth like a dream, sharing his taste...ripe, unique...almost sweet.

He slid his other hand down across her shoulder, leaving a path of fire in the wake of his touch. Rianne moaned as he palmed her breast and tweaked the nipple, tugging it rhythmically. Each time he tugged on her nipple, she could feel an echo of it in her pussy.

He felt so hot against her, and the very air around him simmered with wild magick, so powerful, so elemental. Starving, she chased his tongue with hers as he started to pull away, eagerly trying to draw him back to her.

She quivered as he met her tongue with his, rough and hungry and…different. Everything about him was different—exotic, wild, alien. Her belly quivered as he pulled away, kissing his way down the length of her neck as her head fell back, the long, silken rope of her braid tumbling behind her shoulder, so long it nearly touched the ground.

He lifted his head as he arched her back, running one hand down the center of her torso, his eyes hot, smoking and pinwheeling with sparks of red and gold. "Sweet, hungry thing," he murmured, narrowing his eyes as he shifted, moving back and bringing her to her knees. Then he pushed one knee between her thighs, grinding the hard, muscled length of his thigh against her mound. "I am going to strip you naked and ride you until the moon comes overhead. Then after you rest, I'll do it again."

Rianne whimpered as she stared up at him, her eyes wide and rapt on his face. His hands went to the lacing of her bodice, jerking it free and peeling the skintight garment away, baring her breasts to his eyes. The white globes of her breasts fit perfectly in his palms and he hummed in approval.

"Sweet and perfect. Everything about you is sweet and perfect." Moving to the side, he jerked the rest of her clothing away and reached for the binding on her braid, freeing the black, silken skeins and smoothing the wavy mass until it gleamed around her like a cloak.

Pressing his thumb against her lips, he whispered, "I do think I need to feel this mouth on me, on my cock. Now."

Rianne blinked as he drew her head to him, his eyes unblinking on her face. Licking her lips nervously, she blinked before tearing her eyes away from his face and staring at the hard, thick length of him as he aimed the broad, rounded cock head toward her parted lips. Slowly, she wrapped her lips around him, rolling her eyes to stare up at him before sliding her mouth up and down on his length in a slow, teasing stroke.

"Ummm, that is good," he crooned, rocking his hips forward and driving his length farther inside, nearly gagging her before he withdrew, one hand wrapped around the base of his shaft, marking her limit. His other hand fisted in her hair and guided her into a fast, hungry rhythm. "Bleeding hell, you are perfect," he rasped, driving harder against her lips, nearly bruising.

Curious, Rianne cupped his balls in her hand, pressing the pad of one finger against the smooth area just behind his sac. He felt hot under her hands, his skin smooth, oddly soft. Heat flooded her as he groaned roughly and started to fuck her mouth with short, deep digs. His taste... Keening hungrily in her throat, she licked and suckled at him, craving more of the sandalwood and vanilla taste of him. Heated drops of pre-come spilled from his cock and she suckled harder, desperate for more of it, of him—that wild, foreign taste, the scent of his flesh flooding her mind.

"That's it, sweet, more, just...bloody hell!" a deep, guttural roar tore from his chest, echoing through the woods and sending the forest into silence as he started to come, flooding her mouth with hot, creamy seed, his hand tightening in her hair to the point of near pain.

She swallowed, sucking eagerly until he had emptied himself, pulling her up and away from him with his grip on her hair, keeping his hold on her as he urged her onto her back. He caught her nipple in his mouth and drew it deep, laving the pebbled flesh with his tongue as he pushed her thighs apart. Rianne felt the teasing brush of his cock against her mound and she moaned, arching up to him.

"Slow down," he purred, cupping her hips in his hands. He angled her so that he could stroke his length against her. Each brush of his flesh made her hotter, had her hungrier, until she was rocking against him and pleading with him.

Eilrah laughed, the sound harsh and ragged. "You'll drive me mad," he rasped as he pressed his body against hers, his weight driving her into the ground. He held her gaze as he shifted his angle, pushing against her.

Rianne sobbed as she felt him push inside, just the merest inch. "Fuck me...you're tight," he groaned. His eyes closed as he slid his hands up and linked them with hers, pinning them beside her head.

Then he pushed deep inside her with one long, driving thrust, the taut, wet walls of her sheath stretching tight around him.

Her pain-filled shriek filled the air as he unwittingly tore through virgin tissues. His head whipped up and those fantastic eyes narrowed on her, an odd emotion crossing his face as he slowed his deep, relentless drive into her burning pussy.

"Bloody hell," he groaned, his brow dropping to rest against hers. "A sweet, soft virgin...such wild power inside you, yet you are virgin."

Tears streamed out of her eyes as he moved his mouth to her cheek, licking away the salty tracks before he covered her lips with his, sliding his tongue teasingly into her mouth. Eilrah slowly released her hands as he pushed onto his elbows, taking his weight from her as he pulled out slowly.

"It's all right," he whispered, nuzzling her cheek as he started to thrust gently back inside her wet, convulsing pussy. She whimpered, trying to pull back, sinking into the ground beneath him, away from the stretching, probing length.

"No," Eilrah murmured, regret thick in his voice. "No. Do not pull away, pretty witch."

Rianne slowly sucked in air, trying to breathe past the pain ripping through her lower body. It burned through her, a brutal shock to senses that had just been swimming with pleasure.

She tried to lower her legs and pull away, but one of Eilrah's hands cupped her cheek and the other gripped one of her legs just behind her knee, keeping her locked against him.

He stroked her hair back from her face, lowering his head to nuzzle her neck before pressing a kiss to her earlobe. "Don't pull away," he murmured again. "Sweet Rianne...give me your mouth again."

Her lips trembled under his, opening easily for him even as she tried to clench her thighs together to keep him from moving deeper within her.

"Shhh, relax, trust me," he whispered, his eyes glowing hot and wild in his face. Smoky plumes came from his mouth before he lowered it to hers. The plumes were hot, living things that caressed her body as he drove his tongue into her mouth, his hands sliding down to cup her breast, her hip, stroking up and down the length of her thigh.

The plumes of smoke rolled over her like another set of hands. Eilrah pulled out and surged back in, groaning as the silken, wet sheath relaxed minutely and her breath left her in a weak, broken moan.

"Eilrah," she gasped against his mouth, her hands gripping at the hard, golden curve of his biceps, her thighs lifting, hugging his hips as he sank back inside her cleft, a slick wet glide of his flesh through hers. Her body arched and trembled as ghostly, light hands caressed her arms, her nipples, and her ass.

"That is it, Rianne. My pretty witch, that is it, open for me, give up to me," he crooned, licking a hot, wet trail around her nipple before taking it into his mouth and suckling deep,

161

curling his tongue around it, laving her with slow, unhurried strokes.

Rianne whimpered, a hungry, broken sound that echoed in his ears like glory as he plundered her silky wet depths. One hand slid down, cupping her hip, holding her still as he pulled out, while she reached for him and sobbed. Inch by burning inch, he sank deep inside, a deep, rumbling growl vibrating out of his chest.

"Sweet...hot." A stifled growl left his lips as he cupped her breast, scraping his thumb over her nipple. "You have the sweetest, hottest little pussy...slick and wet." The scent of her need flooded the air and Eilrah felt his control slipping away from him as her nails dug into the firm ridge of muscle at his shoulders.

Pushing up on his elbows, he stared down at her, mesmerized by the sight of her. Her face was flushed, eyes wide and clouded. Thick black locks of hair had come free of her braids, curling around her face, clinging to her neck and shoulders.

"You are so lovely," he whispered, lowering his head to press a kiss to one smoothly rounded shoulder.

Beneath him, she arched, her breasts flattening against his chest, the tissues of her sex clenching around him as she rocked her hips upward.

"Rah...please...help me...oh, there," she sobbed as he rolled his hips against hers and used the friction of his body to tease her clit, over and over, as the need to climax ripped through her.

He could feel it building within her in every wrenching convulsion that tightened her pussy around his cock, could taste it on her skin as she grew hotter, sweeter, spicier under the heated bite of his mouth on her nipples, her neck. "Come for me, pretty little witch. Come..."

His harshly spoken words only served to inflame her more. This was too much, more powerful than any climax she had ever given herself, robbing her of the ability to think, to speak, robbing her of her control. Desperate to regain her control, she clenched her thighs together, tried to pull away, her hands moving to push against his chest.

"Hmmm...too late for that. There is no control left here," he rasped, lowering his lips to the hot, pounding pulse in her throat. "No control. No need to speak, to think, to do anything more than *feel*. Me against you, your sweet, hot little core dripping and writhing around me, each holding the other tight until we burn in the fires of this need. *Feel* it, don't fight it."

"It's too much, too hot," she gasped, jerking her head back even as her hips lifted against his.

"Yes..." he grunted against her throat. "Let it burn you. Burn me in return." After one last scrape of his teeth down her throat, he rose to his knees and grasped her thighs, pushing them wide, opening her for his thrusts, for his eyes, for his magick. Watching her through hooded eyes, he breathed out a plume of smoke, the dragon's touch solidifying as it drifted down her body, centering on her clit and circling it with hard, firm strokes that had her wailing, arching her back as he sank deeper into her slick, sweet cleft. "That is it, my pretty witch..."

As the spasms started to rock her body, tightening her sex around him almost painfully, Eilrah threw his head back and trumpeted his own pleasure to the sky as he started to come, hot splashes of his speed flooding her core. She screamed, locking down on his cock and coming, her eyes glowing, her hands tearing the ground beneath her as the very air around them erupted with flaming sparks and wild magick that painted their bodies with a rainbow of colors.

Her eyes widened, then fluttered as he drove into her one final time, his body gleaming with a misty red light, his amber and red eyes glowing hotly.

As he sank down to collapse on her body, his head resting just below her breasts, he murmured, "That...is a pleasure worth dying for."

* * * * *

Rianne was still shuddering with the aftershocks when they sensed the priestess. Her lips curled up and she murmured, "I wonder what your lovely priestess will make of this."

To her surprise, he flushed, his eyes moving away from her face as he pulled out with a wet, sucking sound that had her gut clenching and her eyes darkening with hunger. "Lady witch," he murmured. "Eiona calls me. I must go..."

"She is coming here. Nearly here—" Then she stopped in mid-sentence as she focused on his face, his expression. "You do not wish her to see you with me." The words were flatly stated. Moving out from under him, she narrowed her eyes at his silence and fought not to let the hot punch of pain show on her face. Rianne was accustomed to rejection.

Though she had never faced it in such a way as this.

Never expected it from the powerful red dragon.

A slow, disgusted smile tugged at her lips. Perhaps the dragon only mated with creatures worthy of his touch. Perhaps she was too wild, too unfocused, too *witchlike* for him. None of her power was as divine as Eiona's, although she far overshadowed the priestess.

Her power was hot, elemental, nothing like the blessed touch she knew the priestess of the earth carried. Rianne's power was so devastating it had damn near gotten her exiled. None of her teachers had wanted anything to do with her, so frightened were they of the power they saw within her.

Too uncontrolled.

Too wild.

Too unclean.

"Go to your priestess, Red Dragon. Do not worry, she will learn nothing from me," Rianne said distantly. A cold, cleansing wind tore through the clearing, blowing away the scents of hot, rich sex. Taking her clothing in one hand, and her staff in the other, she turned away.

"Rianne—"

She stopped, glancing at him over her naked shoulder, feeling his come wet on her thighs, her tender tissues raw and aching from their loving.

"I wish to see you again," he rumbled as the dragon's power tore through him, forming a fine red mist just above his golden skin.

"That is a pity," she said flatly.

As the dragon emerged from the mortal coil, she walked away. Better her than him.

* * * * *

Eilrah sensed the pain inside her as she walked away, but he was unable to move, his hands digging into the earth as the power arced through him, taking his mortal coil and tearing it apart, as the dragon's scaled form erupted. *Damn it, should have waited…*

He couldn't go after her until the change was done with him, couldn't determine that odd, cold light that had moved through her eyes, or its cause. Not yet.

And be damned if she thought he was through with her.

"Dragon, do you not hear me?" Eiona called from somewhere close. Too close. He grunted as the last bits of magick faded and he could move, his black, leathery wings spreading wide as he shifted and stretched. It was odd, though, it wasn't so wonderful to be in this form again. Normally leaving the mortal coil behind once he had satisfied the lust, he wanted nothing more than to feel the air beneath his wings as he launched himself into the sky.

The need to mate was normally unwanted, unwelcome. A bothersome scratch he must satisfy in order to be satisfied in his true form.

165

Yet, all he truly wanted just now was to bring Rianne back, and hold her in his mortal arms.

"Bloody hell, dragon, there you are. Is sunning your ever lovely hide so damn important?" Eiona asked as she strode into the clearing, her black brows drawn low over her gleaming eyes. "You are needed back at the village."

"I sense nothing wrong, other than your incessant chattering," he said, scowling as he thought of going to the village. He arched his head, staring through the woods, wondering if he could catch up with Rianne before she reached her lands, and cuddle that sweet, soft body against his before he shifted back to mortal form and mounted her.

He yearned to feel her hands against him, stroking the powerful flex of his wings, his gleaming red form, before he shifted to his other form and urged her to her knees before him, thrusting his cock into her sweet, tasty mouth.

"I didn't say anything was wrong. You are wanted, Eilrah. Let's go already," she said impatiently, flicking her short black hair out her eyes.

"Oh, do hush," he groused.

There would be no chasing after Rianne just yet.

His priestess, his friend had need of him.

But he was more interested in satisfying *his* needs. For the first time in ages, the need to listen to his heart felt more necessary than listening to his priestess.

Of course, it was rather odd.

Usually his priestess and his heart spoke the same to him.

Chapter Three

ஓ

Rianne sat in the tree, watching carefully as the neangral male approached the female. The neangrals had always been scarce, but they weren't breeding well of late. It had been several years since a new litter had been born.

If this male didn't successfully mate this female, there would be no breeding mates for the older generation of youth and the males might hunt out their own siblings to mate on, causing weakness in future generations.

Which is where Rianne would have to interfere by herding the wild, ferocious cats away from each other, into other lands where they might find mates. The ferocious cats were needed here—badly. They preyed on the more feral creatures of the woods, including the roaming *Saphicates* that were hunting more and more freely.

But they were rather protective of the humans. Making humans and neangrals excellent bedmates, so to speak.

But the males were rough when they mated. Sometimes too rough and the female took offense, slashing out with her deadly claws and tearing away from the male. Her smaller form would allow her to take refuge in the trees, where she would hide until her fertile period was over.

Ahh...these animals were just not stupid enough. Most other female animals took the male's mounting regardless of how rough he might be.

Next to the humans, the neangral were the most intelligent, and demanded a more...sensitive mating. As in no drawing of blood during the act.

So far, the male was being very...polite, urging his mate to the ground and mounting her, keeping his claws sheathed, and his deadly teeth gentle as he nipped at her back.

The scent of the cats' musk drifted through the clearing and Rianne shifted, feeling the hungry urges rising in her. Watching the mating of the cats was a wild, erotic vision. But she somehow doubted that stroking herself to orgasm after her job was done would satisfy her.

The male had ridden the female to ground, and a pleased, throaty growl left him as he drove inside her.

That was when she scented it. Isha growled from his spot at the base of the tree, his hackles rising. *Saphicate*, he said angrily. *It hunts the mating pair.*

Rianne had to keep the *Saphicate* away from the pair.

And she had to do it before the male realized they were in danger. He would become aggressive, and the female would flee before the male had bred her fully.

Saphicate killing the big cats, Isha said, his mind voice throbbing and full of fury, so much so it washed her vision red. She could see images in his mind that he had gleaned from the *Saphicate's* mind and she fought the urge to scream out her fury.

How did I miss this? she thought, enraged.

The *Saphicates* were hunting the neangral to extinction, keeping them from breeding. Isha showed her how many times this *Saphicate* had given away his presence to the male, just before the completion of the breeding, bringing out the rage inside the male, causing the male to claw and bite and the female to strike back before she fled to the safety of the trees, her lighter, slimmer form keeping her safe and secure, her mate earthbound.

No breeding, no babies. And the neangral would die off in this area, leaving the villagers without their protection.

She dropped to the ground soundlessly, hoping the male would recognize her scent and feel safe as he rutted.

When no alarm sounded from the female, Rianne assumed she was safe to continue. Butting her staff against the ground, she whispered quietly. The other hand lifted, palm out, as she sighted the ring of trees around the small clearing. A fine, misty barrier simmered to life, and Rianne checked it completely.

"That will work rather well," she murmured. Now that something would keep the *Saphicate's* stink from reaching the neangral, she locked in on the beast moving through her forest. The barrier would keep the *Saphicate* well away from the mating pair, both by scent, by sight, by touch. Leaving him to Rianne.

* * * * *

Eiona knelt behind a tree, her eyes locked on the blue-skinned *Saphicate* that was still unaware of her presence.

Kye knelt at her back, a silent, watchful shadow. She could feel his tension. It was a wonder the entire forest didn't feel his tension.

Eilrah circled in the sky above, his sharp anger flooding her.

The murdering bastards were destroying the neangral. And Eiona knew bloody well why. They thought if they destroyed the cats that lived at the borders of the village, then the village would easily be wiped out.

"They do not think a priestess is much of a threat, do they, Eilrah?"

His sarcastic laugh echoed in her mind and overhead he bugled. "My priestess is much threat. I'm rather insulted they aren't so worried about us. They did go after the witch. But they have left us alone. How insulting."

She glanced over her shoulder and saw that Kye had glanced up at Eilrah. She smiled a little as Kye asked, "*And how do you know that they went after the witch?*"

"Why, because I watched it. She handles herself so very well," Eilrah responded.

Kye grinned. "I would imagine so. She is a fighter."

"Indeed," Eilrah replied. "Indeed…"

Eiona arched a brow. There was something odd in his voice there. Something very…different. Pride…something more. Something she couldn't quite decipher.

She knew her dragon well, as well as he knew her.

This was odd.

Creeping out from behind the tree, and working their way to another, Eiona and Kye watched the blue skin as the beast moved closer and closer to the clearing where Eiona could scent the mating pair.

She had reached for her blade when something moved in front of her.

Eiona hadn't even sensed the witch.

And the witch was already moving up behind the *Saphicate*, her staff held at ready as she stood, straightening.

"Damn her, she's going to fight a *Saphicate* fairly? Call him out?" Eiona said, shaking her head. "She is a lunatic."

There was no answer from the sky, but she could feel fury rising from Eilrah. Kye simply responded, *"I think our witch knows what she is doing, love."*

But Eiona doubted that. She could scent more *Saphicates* moving in. Moving in to kill, to feast on the flesh of the great cats.

"Are the two of you going to sit there, priestess? Or fight these scavengers?" Rianne's calm, casual voice rang out through the forest and the *Saphicate* whirled, wheeled around on his heel and launched himself at Rianne. "Ahhh…now you see me, do you, bastard?"

The *Saphicate* hissed and struck out with a clawed hand but Rianne countered with her staff, hitting the creature in the belly and whispering as she hit him. The blunt end of it tore

170

through the thick hide of the *Saphicate* and she started to speak, her eyes gleaming with triumph as she invoked the old language.

Eiona could barely recognize the archaic command. Something to do with a cutting fire…and then her eyes fell to the *Saphicate* which lay in two pieces, the corpse smoking as Rianne drew her staff back.

Eilrah winged down, his massive feet landing lightly on the ground. He bugled and fire spat from his nostrils, streaming across the clearing and setting fire to the first *Saphicate* to tear through the woods and try to join his sibling. Eiona stood, drawing her blade from her hip and slicing her palm. Blood flowed and welled, spilling to the ground as Eiona whispered, "Show yourselves to us."

The snarling, angry hisses around them numbered six. Eilrah spewed fire at the tightest concentration of them, incinerating three.

Kye drew his sword and struck at the one to his left, his long form weaving a deadly pattern around the *Saphicate* as he lured the creature away from the others.

That left Eiona to handle the one at her back. She ducked and rolled just as he lunged for her. She struck up with her knife and gutted him as he flew over her, his light, wiry body seeming to hover in mid-air.

Hot, foul blood splattered her face.

She was still spitting it out when the laughter rang in the air. Rising to her feet, she saw the witch facing off with the last *Saphicate*, the largest, most powerful of them and there was a wide grin on her face, her dark blue eyes lit with an unholy light.

"Come and get me, bastard," she snarled in the hissing tongue of the *Saphicate*.

"With pleasure, witch."

Eilrah exploded into full-size form and the dying hiss of a *Saphicate* filled the air as two clawed hands gripped the

Saphicate and tore him into pieces, throwing the carcass to the ground and blasting the stinking pieces to ashes. Eiona stumbled as the red rage that flooded her dragon spilled over into her, tightening her throat, hooking her hands into claws.

"Eiona, block him off," said a firm, commanding voice. "He can handle his rage alone, but if you lose yourself in it, you are both in trouble."

She could hear Kye speaking to her, felt his hands, firm and strong on her arms, but still—she couldn't do as he demanded. Couldn't block the dragon out—rage tore through her and she threw back her head, screaming.

"Eiona!" This time, Kye's voice sounded desperate, almost panicked.

"Let me try, Kye," a soft, gentle voice interrupted.

Kye's hand fell away and Eiona tried to turn and run away, but new hands held. Smaller, softer, but still strong, keeping her from moving away.

She struck out at the hands on her arms, but it did little good. A cool hand, soft and sizzling with power cupped her chin and she felt the power slide over her, through her, separating her from the rage of the dragon. When her eyes cleared, Eiona was standing with her back to a tree as Rianne stared at her with dark, turbulent eyes.

"Have mercy," Eiona whispered weakly, the strength leaving her. She would have sagged to the ground, but Kye moved up, catching her body against him.

"Your dragon needs you. Go to him, calm him," the witch ordered.

Eiona didn't think she could.

The rage inside Eilrah was massive, more than she had felt from him in a very long time, and she had been unprepared for it.

But as she stared at the dragon, eyeing the fine red mist above his scales, the flittering bits of flame that escaped him every time he breathed out, the flames dying before they hit the ground, she knew she had better calm him.

"Eilrah," she said, her voice shaking. Scowling at her weakness, she firmed her voice and bellowed out the dragon's name, infusing it with every bit of power she had inside her.

With Kye at her side, she moved to Eilrah, praying she could keep his rage locked out. "Eilrah," she said, her voice gentle and low. Carefully, she reached out to lay one hand on the smooth glistening scales, feeling the heat from him, the pulsing, pounding power of his rage. Wind blew back from her face as she flooded him with her magick, the magick of the earth, the soothing, restful essence of it.

Slowly, the heat died and when she blinked up at him, the rage eased and a breath shuddered through him as he drew into himself, returning to the smaller form he preferred to inhabit. The red-streaked, golden eyes met hers but she couldn't read the look there.

It looked too…human.

* * * * *

Eilrah could hardly breathe as Rianne melted into the forest while he incinerated the rest of the corpses.

Wait…he growled into her mind.

She jerked at his mental touch, surprised for the briefest moment.

Shaking her head, she said, "Your priestess is here. Remember?"

Eilrah felt Eiona's eyes on him, the puzzlement in his priestess's soul. She was the other half of his soul, hers a mirror to his. But she had never known him to have such *human* feelings, and they were alien.

But as Rianne walked away from him, he could only stand there and watch, tearing at the earth with restless claws.

Wishing with all his heart that he could go after her.

Eiona's presence kept him locked in place and for the first time, he found himself resenting the bond that held them so tightly together.

* * * * *

Eiona lay under Kye, still gasping for air as he lowered his body and collapsed against her, one cheek resting in the valley between her breasts, his long, dark red hair spread around them and covered their bodies like a cape.

"Now that I have gotten that out of my system," he rasped, stroking his fingers down her side. "Why don't you tell me what's bothering you, babe?"

Eiona's mouth twitched. Even after eleven years, he carried much of the speech from his former life. *Babe, honey, darlin'…*

She really liked darlin', the way it flowed from his sensuous, sexy mouth like a caress.

"Can a dragon fall in love, I wonder?"

Kye's body tensed as he lifted up, planting one elbow on either side of her hips. His gleaming eyes widened and he said, "That certainly wasn't what I expected to hear." A thoughtful frown firmed his mouth as he rubbed one thumb back and forth over her ribcage and thought about it. "Eilrah has so much of you inside, darlin', his thoughts and your thoughts are too often one. I can't say it's the most peaceful thing. Especially if he is out hunting, or full of restlessness. I can see his emotions through you. I guess it's not too far a stretch of the imagination for him to feel the more human emotions."

She understood his odd turns of phrase now…even though from time to time, she still had to stop and think it through. "And if he is falling in love with a human, what does that mean for him besides heartbreak? How can he have a life like that? He is dragon."

"You're talking about Rianne."

Eiona's mouth curved in a slight smile. "You saw how he was with her—it was the threat to her that enraged him so." She glanced down at him with an arched brow. "The very picture of a man who's lover has been threatened."

Kye grinned at her. His hair, that deep warm red, spilled over his shoulder as he pushed up onto his elbow. "It was a little weird. Eilrah is the picture of calm and rationality."

"Not today, he wasn't," Eiona murmured. "He is dragon. He shouldn't feel what we feel."

"Yes. But he shares your heart, your head, your feelings. If he isn't supposed to fall in love with a human, then he won't," Kye said, shrugging his shoulders and lowering his head back to her breasts. "Things happen for a reason, Eiona. They always happen for a reason."

She sighed, wrapping her arms around his neck, holding him close to her. "I don't like her, Kye. I don't trust her."

Kye scowled. "Rianne?" he asked flatly.

"Yes."

"Why don't you trust her?" he asked as he rolled off her, again rising up on his elbow to stare down at her with dark eyes.

"She is uncontrollable, Kye," she said softly. "I know she experienced something terrible. But...but perhaps it scarred her inside, broke something. How do we know she can control herself?"

"*I* know." Kye stood and turned away from her, staring into the fire. "I know she can. I remember the girl she was, Eiona. She was a sweet, gentle little kid. The bastards who destroyed Miden School deserved to die. I will not fault her for that."

Eiona sighed, sitting up and drawing her knees to her chest. Resting her chin there, she said quietly, "I do not fault her for what she did there. But that doesn't mean I can trust what she has become."

"You're wrong."

Eiona stilled, lifting her gaze to find him staring at her with chilly eyes. He hadn't ever told her that before—oh, Eiona knew she was wrong often enough, but he usually let her come to that conclusion on her own.

"I hope I am," she said stiltedly. "But that's not the point here. My point is…Eilrah. What am I to do?"

"You don't have to do anything."

Eiona rolled her eyes and stood up. "Bloody hell, I don't. That is my companion, my brother in soul. I cannot even understand why he feels anything for her, much less understand what I sense from him."

Kye shrugged. "I do."

"You do?" she asked. Narrowing her eyes, she stared into the fire, crossing her arms over her breasts. "You understand?"

"She's beautiful. She's strong. She's powerful. If he is having mortal emotions, well, Eilrah is male and he picked a good female to focus on."

Jealousy pricked at her. Glaring at him over her shoulder, she said, "She's not a good female. She hides in the forest all the time, she never speaks to anybody, and she's too powerful. Too unpredictable."

Kye snorted. "You admitted that you can understand why she hides." Propping his hands on his hips, he added, "Hiding in the forest, never speaking to anybody…you do realize who that sounds like."

Eilrah. Closing her eyes, she whispered, "Kye, she's human. He's dragon. It can't work."

She heard him sigh and looked at him, seeing the frustration on his face melt away as he drew near. He wrapped his arms around her, pulling her back against him.

"Stop worrying about him so much. He can take care of himself—and even if he's walking into heartbreak, he's a big boy. He makes his own choices."

Leaning her head back against his shoulder, she let him cuddle her closer. "Why her? She has changed so much since she left here."

"She was a child when she left," Kye murmured. "She grew up. And she's faced more heartbreak than any person should have to face. She's sad, baby. You can see it in her eyes."

Blowing out a breath, she said, "Yeah. I know."

Chapter Four

ᔓ

Eilrah was fucking furious as he stalked through the woods. Not only had she not waited for him, she was evading him. Bad enough he had to watch as the powerful *Saphicate* faced her, daring to *think* of harming her, but now he couldn't get his hands on her and reassure himself that she was well, whole, hearty…unaffected by the poison of the *Saphicate's* blood.

It had been more than a day since he had watched her walk away from him and he couldn't find her.

You shouldn't have let her walk away, he thought, furious with himself. *Should have followed her, stayed with her…*

Eiona hadn't needed him.

But Rianne had. She had needed him—*him*, not the great Red Dragon. And he'd be damned if he lost that.

But he couldn't even find her.

Damn it, what if she is not immune? he thought desperately. If the poison had affected her… The images that thought brought to mind had him trembling with fury and terror. The poison could have eaten through her skin and by now. She could be lying frozen, easy prey for so many predators.

"Rianne!"

A soft sigh seemed to surround him and her voice echoed from all around. "What do you want, Red Dragon? Aren't you a little far from your home? Your priestess?"

"Eiona and I do not cage the one another. If she has need of me, I will know." Driving his hands through his hair, he bellowed, "Come out, Rianne. Come to me."

The wind whistled up around him, blowing his hair back from his face as a small dust storm formed in front of him, solidifying until Rianne stood in before him, her head cocked, a curious smile on her face. "I am here, Red Dragon. Whatever are you bellowing about?"

The relief that shot through him evaporated at her words. "My name...you know my name and it is not *Red Dragon*. Say my name," he rasped, reaching up and cupping the back of her neck in his hand and jerking her against him.

"What has you so heated up?" she drawled, her voice sarcastic, her lip poking out slightly.

"My name. I have a name, and it's not *Red Dragon*. I am *more* than just the priestess's dragon. I am Eilrah, a man who wants you," he growled against her lips.

"But you aren't a *man*. You only take this form when you feel like it," she replied coolly, turning her face aside.

Eilrah growled, lowering his head and pressing his lips to her ear. "Wrong. I *have* to take this form, and sometimes more often than I would choose. It's an ache inside of me that I cannot rid myself of, the need to be *man*, and not dragon. To do things as a man would. My feelings are those of a man, not those of a *dragon*. Dragons don't lust for mortal women. A dragon doesn't yearn for the feel of soft skin against his, or need to feel a woman's heat enveloping his sex. I *crave* these things. I have to have them...and you. I have to have you."

She ignored the hungry, yearning look in his eyes as she shoved against his chest, unable to move though. His hands gripped her hips, holding her firm against him. "But only when your priestess doesn't call for you. Go and sate your needs with her."

"With Eiona? Are you mad? She is my priestess...it would be like having sex with myself," he growled, walking her back up against a tree and angling his hips so that he could pump his aching cock against her belly.

"Go and have sex with yourself, then, and leave me be," she hissed, jerking her head back yet again and evading his mouth. "I won't be second best to another."

"What in the bloody hell are you talking about?" he demanded.

"You hear her call and you take off running, leaving me behind, cold and alone," she snapped, her eyes wide and gleaming with the hurt he hadn't realized he had inflicted.

Stilling, he whispered, "I am sorry." Memories of their one time together leaped to his mind, and he remembered the odd, shuttered look on her face as she had walked away.

He hadn't understood.

But now...sighing, he pressed his forehead to hers and whispered again, "I am sorry." He licked his lips, suddenly nervous as he tried to find the words to explain why he hadn't wanted Eiona to see him with Rianne.

He should have told Eiona long before now, but until recently, it had always been a bother, an inconvenience that he did not want.

One that had come on him because of his bond with her.

Finally, he lifted his head and met Rianne's chilly gaze. "I did not mean to hurt you. It is just...Eiona doesn't know."

"Doesn't know what?" she asked suspiciously.

"Of this," he answered, gesturing to himself. His thick black hair fell into his eyes and he added, "I have simply never thought of the right way to tell her."

Rianne's eyes widened as they swept over the handsome, very mortal form in front of her. "You are surely jesting..." her voice trailed off as she studied his eyes. "How can you not have told her?"

Stroking his thumb across the satiny skin of her cheek, he said, "At first, I didn't know how to handle this form. It overtook me, the magick that lets it happen. I felt it the first time and just accepted it, not knowing what it was. It was a part of me, and I knew it wouldn't hurt me. But I didn't realize it was going to change me. I'd been...restless for months and it built and built until it took me over and just exploded. When the magick passed, I was like this. I did not know what to make of it. At first, I feared I was losing my mind.

"And the needs that brought the change on, until I learned how to control it, they were...obsessive. I didn't want to be around her while I was fighting to control the urges as well as the change. When I finally stopped fighting it, it became easier. Then I simply didn't know how to approach it. It felt like a curse—at first. And it happened because of the bond I share with her...Eiona. I did not want to burden her with this." The red pinwheels in his dark eyes flashed, shifting and sparking as he spoke. "It's not exactly something that you would expect to see, not anything I ever expected to happen."

"What brings it on?" she asked suspiciously, the look in her eyes telling him she already suspected what it was.

Pulling her lower body up snug against his aching cock, he whispered, "This...a need. And right now, I need you." Gathering her hair in his hand, he lowered his mouth to her neck and scored it with his sharp teeth, reveling in the shudder that racked her body. "I had never felt true pleasure, though, until I sank my cock inside your sweet, wet pussy. I understand now why Kye looks so smug, so satiated all the time. If I had you with me at night, able to take you as I please, I'd never stop grinning."

"Dragons don't grin," she said absently, her eyes clouding with lust as he lifted her up against him.

"Do I look dragon now? I am man, and I want my woman," he growled, taking her mouth roughly, thrusting his tongue deep inside, tasting her unique, spicy taste. His hands came up between them and gripped the laces holding her skinsuit together, shredding them and peeling the tight leather away from her naked, proud breasts. Plumping the soft mound of flesh in one hand, he stroked a hard, erect nipple, pinching it between forefinger and thumb while he worked the skinsuit down her hips with the other hand. "My woman," he purred as he kissed his way down her neck, catching a beaded, rosy nipple in his mouth, sucking her deep, laving at the flesh with his rough tongue.

"Rah, this is insanity," she gasped even as she arched up against him, pushing her nipple deeper into his mouth. "We cannot—"

"We will," he argued as he wrapped his arms around her and used his weight to take her to the ground. "Tonight, tomorrow, as often as we can, wherever we can." Giving up on her skinsuit, he shredded it, leaving her bare to his seeking eyes. "You and I will spend eternity together."

"You cannot spend eternity with *me*. You are bound to Eiona."

"In my soul, she is my sister, my self. But you are my world and I will be with you," he swore hotly as he pushed to his knees and spread her thighs wide, watching as he slowly fed his aching length into the warm, waiting core of her, the lips of her sex wet and gleaming. "Feel it, Rianne, and tell me this isn't right."

As his cock forged slowly inside, she whimpered, reaching down and gripping his wrist in one hand. A startled, yearning cry left her lips as he seated himself fully inside her and started to move within her, slow, deep thrusts, stroking over the bundled nerve endings and smiling as she screamed.

Her pussy locked down around his cock, spasming and clenching, milking his climax closer and closer. "Come now, I want to feel you coming on my cock, I want to feel it as the sweet cream pours from your body and I fill you with my seed."

"Rah," she sobbed just as the climax tore through her, abrupt and sudden, uncontrollable. Groaning, he pressed against her, clenching his eyes closed as he fought to hold onto his control.

Slowly, she stilled beneath him and he opened his eyes to stare down at her as he started to ride her once more. "Stay with me," he crooned, stroking one hand down her body, cupping her hip and lifting her against him.

"Stay with me…" He breathed out a single plume of smoke and directed it to glide down her body, watching as the ghostly little plume centered on her clit.

It began to circle and vibrate against the pebbled flesh and he felt her arch up against him, clenching around him and screaming.

The bite of her nails on his shoulder had him grimacing in ecstasy.

Driving harder and harder inside her, groaning at the wet, tight caress of her pussy on his sex, Eilrah lowered his mouth to her breasts, those pretty pink nipples. Sliding his hands under her, he held her steady for his thrusts, driving deep and high inside her, sending her spasming into another climax. The tight, rhythmic caresses of her sensitive tissues and muscles finally shattered his control and he growled, bending his head to take her mouth with his as he shafted her hungrily, greedily.

His sac went white-hot, and hot embers of sensation ripped through him as he started to come, her clenching sheath drawing it from him as she clutched at him, holding him tighter as she wailed and cried out his name.

* * * * *

He fell asleep pressed against her back, one arm wrapped securely around her. Rianne stared sightlessly ahead. Her body ached and her heart felt heavy in her chest. Was this what lay before her? Spending an hour here and there with him, and watching as he walked away from her every time Eiona said his name.

It would be almost as if she had fallen in love with a married man. Almost. But this would be worse. The bond that held Eiona and Eilrah together was likely stronger than any pledge a man could make to a woman. Not even death could break their bond. Closing her eyes, she sighed as a hot tear trickled out from under her lashes.

That left Rianne alone, just waiting for him to return to her from time to time.

And she would wait. She had to be honest with herself— she felt something for this dragon trapped inside a mortal's body, something that went deeper than lust. Deeper than need.

Her eyes flew open as she sensed the priestess enter her forest. Behind her, she felt Eilrah waken, leaning forward to press his lips against her shoulder. He would leave now. She tried to hold herself stiff, praying that would lessen the blow when he rose and left her alone again.

"You always smell so sweet," he muttered, burying his face in her hair and pulling her more firmly against him.

Feeling the hard, heavy press of his cock against her bottom, she closed her eyes against the heat that began to swamp her. "Your priestess is looking for you," she said flatly.

"Let her look," Eilrah murmured as he shifted, rolling her onto her belly and blanketing her body with his.

A harsh, startled moan escaped her as he started to roll his hips against her ass, making those flames burn even hotter. His hands came up, catching hers and pinning them to the ground.

Rianne moaned, digging her knees into the ground and pressing back against him. The cheeks of her ass parted just a little and he smoothed his hand down her side, shifting his weight off of her for a minute as he opened her farther. Then he leaned back into her, rocking back and forth, the head of his cock butting against the tight pucker of her ass.

"I'll take you here," he whispered. "And you will scream...you will scream out my name."

184

There? She opened her mouth to speak but she couldn't, her breath locked in her throat, her heart slamming against her ribs.

From the corner of her eye, she saw him reach out, and pluck her belt from the ground. As he pushed up and knelt behind her, Rianne tried to shift away, but he just placed his hand at the small of her back. "Be still," he ordered gruffly.

The sweet scent of *cacerin* oil filled the air and she glanced over her shoulder, eyes widening as she watched him tilt the bottle he had taken from her belt. Thick, clear oil flowed from it, coating his cock. Using his other hand, he smeared the oil over the hard, thick flesh.

When he reached out and touched her with his oil-slicked hand, she jumped, startled. As he started to rub her with the oil, she tried to squirm away, her face flushing.

"Eilrah, no. You can't...you can't mean to..." words failed her and she slumped down, pressing her flaming face to the ground.

"Aye. I can. And I will," he purred roughly as he started to probe there. As the tip of one finger pushed inside, Rianne cried out. A sharp pain tore through her and she clenched the cheeks of her butt together, trying to keep him from pushing farther inside.

"Relax," he crooned. She felt the telltale heat as he breathed out one of those sinful plumes of smoke and it began to caress her, winding around her body, her nipples, wrapping around her, moving lower and lower. As it started to tease her clit, she sobbed, rocking against that teasing caress.

She felt him press against her again and when he pushed farther inside, she was too focused on the heated caresses on her body to tense up. He circled around, wiggling his finger back and forth, loosening the muscles there as he coated her with more of the oil.

He started to pump his finger in and out and Rianne pushed back to meet him, startled at the hot, wicked delight that spiraled through her. She barely realized the smoky plume wasn't touching her anymore. Just his finger inside her ass, and then another, stretching her bit by bit.

Her clit ached and throbbed. She could feel the orgasm building, circling through her, that tension climbing higher and higher. She felt the touch of his dragon's magick again—this time it felt like a mouth was sucking on her clit even as something hot and solid seemed to push inside her hungry pussy.

She exploded and it was while she was screaming her way through climax that he pushed the fat head of his cock inside her. The circling motions of her hips took him deeper and by the time the climax had passed, she had taken half of his cock inside.

Rianne froze—bracing her hands against the ground, arching her back against the foreign feel of his cock throbbing inside her ass. His hands gripped her hips, holding her in place. Holding her—hell, even if she *tried* to move, she doubted she could. He felt so hot, so thick, stretching her, forcing his way inside her.

He started to pump his hips—just slow, small thrusts, back and forth. Electric little jolts of sensation tore through her and she stiffened, trying to pull away. He tightened his grip on her hips and said gruffly, "No. You've taken this much, you can take more."

His weight crushed her to ground, her hips resting on a slight dip that had her butt angling up. Rianne braced her hands against the earth, shaking her head. "Damn it, Rah. It's too much," she sobbed, clenching the muscles in her bottom.

"Yes," he rumbled against her back. "It is. Feel it…let it burn you like you burn me."

She cried out as he pulled out, then surged deeper inside her. He breathed against her neck and she felt the heat of his breath winding around her. His magick was back, stroking the sides of her breasts, easing under her pinned body to toy with her clit. It felt like a mouth again, teeth nibbling at tender flesh, lips sucking on her, tongue stroking around and around.

And all the while, Eilrah moved into her with steady, unfaltering determination until he was lodged inside her completely, his hips pressed against her ass. "You took it," he whispered unsteadily. "All of me. Now *feel* me."

With deep, slow strokes, he fucked her, filling her ass completely before pulling back out. Rianne cried out with each stroke and slowly she began to rock back as far as she could to meet him. She began to beg for more.

His thrusts became fiercer, more demanding, until he was riding her hard and rough. The phantom mouth feasting on her clit became more avid and she felt the touch of his magick pushing inside her again. Too much sensation, too much heat as he sank into her again, something inside her broke open and she started to scream out his name.

"That's it," he growled as he slammed into her again and again. As he started to come, Rianne was just beginning to come down and she sank bonelessly into the ground. Hot, thick jets of sperm flooded her and then he sank down against her.

A soft call drifted through the woods and Rianne stiffened as she recognized Eiona's voice.

"Where in the hell are you, dragon?"

He grunted, rolling onto his side and taking Rianne with him, cupping his hot body around hers. "She's calling you," Rianne said stiffly.

Eilrah yawned sleepily. "I know. It's nothing urgent—she can wait."

As the voice drifted closer, Rianne couldn't keep the tension from seeping into her body. "She doesn't sound like she wants to wait."

Eilrah made a motion against her back that felt like a shrug. "Eiona has little patience. It's never been one of her stronger virtues but waiting has never killed her."

Eiona drew nearer and her voice was starting to sound irritated. "Damn it, dragon, where in the hell are you?"

Rianne tried to pull away. "Let me go. She's going to be here any second."

Eilrah chuckled. "I wouldn't have pegged you for one of such modesty," he murmured, as he reached over her and grabbed her shawl, flipping the multicolored length over both of them. It only covered Rianne from neck to mid thigh, but that was better than facing the priestess in the nude. Especially since Eilrah wasn't in any hurry to let her go.

"There's a difference between modesty and not choosing to be found naked if you can avoid it," she said sourly, still trying to squirm away from him.

He just laughed and that only served to frustrate her even more. She felt too exposed and it had nothing to do with the lack of clothing. And as Eiona appeared through the trees, the feeling only deepened. She didn't want to face this woman naked, likely stained with grass, tousled…obviously in the arms of her lover.

Her lids drooped as she ran that thought through her mind. Her lover. This powerful, magickal creature was her lover. She just had to wonder, would that be enough to keep him by her side? The bond between Eiona and Eilrah was strong. Too strong.

Eiona came up short and just stood there, staring across the twenty feet that separated her from Eilrah and Rianne. Her eyes flashed, something that looked like fury burning in them before she blanked her expression. "I'm sorry…I didn't expect to find you here." Her eyes moved to Eilrah's face and then back to Rianne's. She barely glanced at Rah, and there was no recognition.

"Who were you expecting to find?"

Rianne could have punched Eilrah as he rumbled out the question. Eiona's eyes met Eilrah's for a second and she replied coolly, "A friend. I apologize for interrupting."

Then she turned on her heel and stalked away.

Rianne jerked away from Eilrah, keeping hold of her scarf and pressing it to her chest as she turned to glare at him. "She doesn't know you."

Eilrah shrugged his shoulders. "No reason she should. She wouldn't expect to see me in any other form than dragon." Rolling onto his back, he closed his eyes, arching his spine and stretching. It was an oddly feline gesture, one she wouldn't have expected from the great Red Dragon. His lashes closed over his eyes and he sighed. "I'll have to speak with her. She was angry over something."

* * * * *

With her face puckered in a scowl, Eiona stalked through the woods.

The fury she felt arcing through her was irrational. She knew that.

Still...she couldn't help it. Eilrah had feelings for that witch, human or no. And Eiona had just found the woman curled in the arms of a man sexy enough to make Eiona's mouth water. And that wasn't easy. Kye had her more than a little picky, but that man...

Who in the hell was he? Did Eilrah know him?

There had been something oddly familiar about him, but she couldn't place him. And it didn't really matter who he was—Rianne had feelings for somebody, and it wasn't Eiona's dragon.

Which added up to just one thing.

Whatever feelings Eilrah had for Rianne, they were wasted. Because Rianne had very, very deep feelings for the man she was with. The emotion hung in the air all around her.

And where in the hell was Eilrah?

She had sensed him there, damn it. She drove a hand through her hair, frustrated beyond all belief. He hadn't ever *not* come when she called.

Eiona was preoccupied. But not so preoccupied that she didn't catch that faint, telltale scent on the wind as she started down a steep incline.

Closing her eyes, she swore hotly.

Damn *Saphicates*. This was too close to the village—far too close.

Even as she shifted direction to move so the wind wouldn't carry her scent to the creatures, she whispered quietly, "Damn it, where are you, dragon?"

Chapter Five

ﾠ

Eilrah's body stiffened and he jackknifed into a sitting position, his eyes staring into the woods.

He didn't have time to even form words as he turned to look at Rianne. She had already rolled to her feet and he saw the knowledge in her eyes.

"They grow bold," she whispered, shaking her head.

"Too bold," Eilrah growled, fury painting the world with a red cast as he grew aware of Eiona's fear.

Surrounded — the damn things had her surrounded.

A trap. She'd walked into a trap while she was out searching for him.

He took off through the forest, his bare feet pounding over the uneven ground. Part of him itched to change, but the hollow where they had trapped Eiona was small, too small for his dragon's form to easily maneuver.

He heard Rianne behind him, her feet moving nearly as fast as his. Part of him was tempted to tell her to stay away, but he knew she'd never listen. Moreover…he would need her.

Through his bond with his priestess, he knew Eiona had counted more than ten *Saphicates*. Ten — spread out and hiding. Unless he wanted to burn the very forest around them down, he couldn't handle ten by himself.

The path in the forest branched off and he took the southern fork, dimly aware that Rianne had taken the northern path. Seconds later, before he had even arrived at his destination, he heard two death screams and the rotting stench of dead *Saphicate* filled the air.

A ferocious smile of pride lit his face for just a minute. The damned scavengers would have their hands full, trying to handle his witch.

My witch...

Reaching out with his mind, he whispered to her, *Stay safe, Rianne. I'll not have what is mine harmed.*

He heard her soft snort as he slowed to a halt. He smiled coolly. She could laugh and snicker about it all she wanted, but she was his. The fierce streak of protectiveness wasn't one he could deny, even if he tried.

And speaking of protectiveness...he reached out with his mind, sensing that Kye had felt Eiona's fear and was already tearing through the forest to reach her.

But would he get there in time? Ten to three were not good odds.

Well, eight to three. The two Eiona had taken out helped lessen those odds just a bit.

Through the dense foliage ahead, he caught sight of a blue-skinned male moving closer to the hollow. Three had already descended and he could sense Eiona preparing to fight.

Spying a small rock in the sloping path, he gave it a small nudge and as it started to roll down the hill, the *Saphicate* whirled.

Eilrah smiled and as the monstrous creature moved closer, he lunged for the *Saphicate*. Taking it to the ground, he opened his mouth and let the fire roar from him, burning the thing beneath him to ashes.

* * * * *

The relief that filled Eiona was indescribable. Although she couldn't see him, she knew Eilrah was here. She sensed him and the destructive element of fire as several of the

Saphicates surrounding her turned to the south, snarling up toward the ridge and hissing in anger.

A pillar of smoke appeared briefly and she smiled. Subtlety hadn't ever been one of Eilrah's strong suits.

Cutting her eyes to the *Saphicate* closest to her, she murmured briefly under her breath. An ominous cracking sound echoed through the forest and the *Saphicates* all searched for the source. As the massive giant oak came crashing to the ground, it caught two of the *Saphicates* under its bulk while several more scattered, narrowly avoiding a crushing death.

More death screams came from the southern ridge and Eiona felt the power of the witch with mixed emotions. Help was welcome…even if Eiona didn't want the witch near her dragon.

The strong, unmistakable scent of sulfur filled the air again and Eiona watched from the corner of her eye as two forms lit in flame. A thundering shout filled the air and she searched quickly for Eilrah, but she couldn't see him. Where he could hide that bulk of his here, she didn't know.

And even as agile and graceful as he was, something as large as he couldn't move undetected through the woods. Where—

A high-pitched scream sounded, cut abruptly short.

Whirling, Eiona stared up at the southern ridge, frozen still for a heartbeat. She forced her legs to move, dodging around a *Saphicate* as it tore from the forest, sliding her blade into the thick hide and jerking. As hot blood gushed out, she dodged away and continued up the hill.

Ahead of her…she saw a man. His body was long and golden, completely nude. Without a doubt, she knew it was the man she'd seen with Rianne. A *Saphicate* lunged for him and the man caught him, closing one hand around the throat, the other grabbing the two-legged predator at its crotch and hurling it in the air.

As the *Saphicate* went flying, flame engulfed it and its remains were nothing but ashes by the time they drifted down to earth. Fire—the unmistakable scent of sulfur. Even as a soft voice whispered inside her mind, she shoved it away.

He disappeared over the ridge and Eiona followed, nearly crashing into his body moments later.

His heat nearly scalded her as she stepped away, following the man's eyes to where Rianne lay on the ground, her eyes wide with pain, blood staining red the green skinsuit she wore. One *Saphicate* knelt at her neck, trailing deadly claws along her pale flesh and three more surrounded them.

The one kneeling beside Rianne spoke, staring at Eiona with an evil smile. "The witch dies—these lands are ours. Your young are ours."

Then the monster lifted his claws, licking away the blood that stained his skin with clear delight. "We will feast on her flesh, and then yours."

She felt more of them moving up behind her and Eiona lifted terrified eyes to stare at the man at her side.

She blinked in astonishment as she saw him through a mist of red.

Not rage, but an actual mist, a glittering red cloud that surrounded his entire body. His eyes moved to hers and shock tore through her as she truly looked into his eyes.

This is not possible… The thought circled through her mind even as she recognized those eyes, the eyes of the other part of her, her brother in soul.

"Step back," he said, his voice a deep bass rumble.

Eiona barely even realized what she was doing but she listened. When two clawed hands tried to grab her, she struck out with her own minor magick and the *Saphicate* went flying.

The red mist grew thicker and thicker until she couldn't make out the form inside it.

A trumpeting roar filled the air, shaking the very earth around them and Eiona turned, diving for the slope. As she started to run down it, the very earth around her seemed to explode.

Trees went flying, dust filled the air.

And when it cleared, she was lying on her back in the hollow, staring up the slope with wide, disbelieving eyes.

* * * * *

Eilrah screamed as the change washed over him, his skin tearing apart and reforming into glittering hard scales. He lashed out with one claw and caught the two *Saphicates* who had been standing over Rianne's wounded body.

Their blood spilled hot on his scales as he crushed them in his claws. Rising on his hindquarters, he stared down at the leader who crouched over Rianne's body. The thing dug his claws into tender white flesh and hissed, "She dies!"

"No," Eilrah rumbled raising one claw and watching as fire swarmed through the air. The *Saphicate* raised his hands to cover his face, shoving back away from Eilrah in terror.

Once the thing was far enough from Rianne, Eilrah spat fire at him. He didn't even watch as the *Saphicate* died, his scream fading as the fire incinerated him in seconds. Just to his left, he sensed more and he turned his head, blasting the trees that hid the *Saphicates*. Screams rose, then died before they fully formed.

He heard the scrambling of bodies to his right and breathed more fire. More and more until everything in front of him was charred and blackened. Everything but the small circle of earth where Rianne lay.

Sinking to the ground, he lifted one massive claw, letting it hover above her body for one moment before jerking away. "Rianne..."

Her eyes opened and she stared at him, her gaze clouded from pain. A gentle smile curved her lips and then she closed her eyes again. A deep shudder racked her and as Eilrah stared helplessly, blood started to trickle from her mouth.

Kye got to her side as she was scrambling back up the hill. It was slow going—somehow, she had wrenched her knee and every time she put weight on that leg, the abused joint screamed in agony.

"Here," he murmured, scooping her into his arms. She glanced up at him and saw his eyes were hot and angry, his mouth a firm, tight line. "I thought we had discussed this—you weren't going to mess with the *Saphicates* alone."

She forced out a pained smile. "Then somebody should have told them that, lover. I was just looking for Eilrah."

Kye blew out a breath, pressing his lips to her temple as his arms tightened around her painfully. "Then maybe I won't strangle you…"

His voice trailed away as they topped the hill and stared out in front of them.

"Heavens above have mercy," Eiona whispered.

The scene that lay before them looked like the aftermath of some terrible battle. A few blackened, charred husks, trees burnt nearly to the ground, smoke rising from the scorched earth.

Kye gently lowered her to the ground and she stood with her weight balanced on her uninjured leg, bracing herself for the worst. Eilrah lay on the ground, his massive body looking terribly broken. He swung his head her way, staring at her with grief in his jewel-like eyes.

"Their poison is in her blood. I can taste it in the air." A huge sigh racked his body and his lids drooped, hiding that heartbroken gaze from her. "She said witches were immune."

Eiona limped around Eilrah, her hands already rooting in the pouches she wore at her waist. "Not completely, just far more resistant," she said tightly. The *echre* root would make her bleed more, but they needed to get that poison out of her system. "If it enters directly into the bloodstream, it can harm a witch just as easily as anyone else."

She crumbled the dry root into a coarse powder, applying it to the nasty wound in Rianne's side. It went deep, but the blood still freely flowing would help for now. As she worked the powder of the root into the wound, blood began to pulse from Rianne's side, thinner and thinner.

"I need something to pack her wound with," Eiona said a few minutes later. "Something to bind it with."

Eilrah just sighed, his massive sides quivering. "Too much blood...she's witch, but still human. Humans cannot lose so much blood."

The despair in his voice damn near broke Eiona's heart, and the blackness she felt rolling from him almost made her throat lock up. Blocking him off, she snapped, "Move, dragon. *Now*. I'll save your woman if you let me, but you had better help."

Chapter Six

ഇ

He could feel the speculative eyes on him as he paced back and forth in front of the lodge Eiona and Kye shared.

It had been hours since Eiona had entered the lodge, leaving him outside alone with Kye.

Back at the ridge, while Eiona had worked over Rianne's body, Kye had stared at him for one second and then shaken his head. "I'll be damned," was all the man had said.

Kye hadn't said anything since. Even when they'd arrived at the village, he'd said nothing. Kye had disappeared for a few minutes then returned to shove some clothes into Eilrah's arms.

The fabric felt foreign against his skin, but he had enough people staring at him curiously. Standing there completely naked wouldn't make it any better.

"What is taking so long?" he growled.

Kye said quietly, "Healing can be a slow process, Eilrah. You know that."

Yes. Yes, he knew. But he hadn't ever felt so helpless before, so useless.

He could feel Eiona's presence—calm, soothing—and it was the only thing that kept him from snarling with rage. If she was calm, then all was well.

It was a litany he kept up. And occasionally, he even had faith in it. But as the day turned into night, his patience dwindled.

Finally, the door to the lodge swung open and Eiona stood there, her face gray with exhaustion, her body swaying.

She gave him a weary smile. "She'll live. If she hadn't been a witch, there was no way I could have saved her. But she will live."

Kye came and took his weary wife in his arms, supporting her weight against his body. She took one limping step and Kye swept her up in his arms, cradling her against him.

He started to move away and she glanced over Kye's shoulder at Eilrah. "I would like an explanation...at some point."

He gave her a terse nod and then disappeared inside the dark maw of the door. Too confining, these human dwellings. How did they tolerate it?

He licked lips gone dry with fear, forcing the inconsequential thoughts from his mind as he drew closer to Rianne. She was *pale*. Terribly pale and still. He crouched down by the bed and trailed the tips of his fingers along her arm. She felt so cold.

Even as he thought it, she shivered, and a gasp of pain escaped her. Her eyes opened, one hand flying protectively to her injured side. At the sight of those blue eyes, Eilrah felt the fist around his heart loosen just a little and he was able to breathe.

"You hurt," he murmured hoarsely.

Her gaze drifted up, meeting his. She smiled sleepily and whispered, "A little. Your priestess does a fine job of healing."

Eilrah closed his eyes, lowering his brow to rest on the edge of the bed as he offered up a prayer of thanks. "Yes. Yes, she does. Thank God."

She tried to tug the blanket tighter around her and Eilrah shifted, resting one arm across her hips, warming her with his body. She seemed to curl into him, sighing with satisfaction. "I've been so cold," she whispered. "Will you stay with me?"

He caught her hand in his and lifted it to his lips, pressing a gentle kiss there. "Always."

Rianne smiled at him, but her eyes looked a little sad. "Be careful—I may hold you to that."

Eilrah reached up, and brushed back her tangled hair. "I am not going anywhere, Rianne. I doubt even death could tear me from you. When I saw you—" his voice broke and Eilrah feared for one moment that he might weep. "When I saw you lying there, I thought I would lose you. There was so much blood, and I wanted to die. I cannot live without you."

Her eyes gleamed with the sheen of tears. "You hardly know me, Rah," she whispered softly.

He caught one of her hands in his, lifted it to his lips and pressed a gentle kiss to the back of it. "I know you. I know your soul. And you know mine. Can you tell me that you do not?"

Her lashes lowered over her eyes and Eilrah felt cold as his heart started to sink like a stone in his chest. Then she looked back up at him, a shaky smile on her lips.

"No. No, I cannot tell you that." She curled closer to him, closing her eyes. "I've been cold a long time, Rah. You're the only man who has ever warmed me."

"I plan on being the *only one* for the rest of our lives," he whispered. "I am not letting you go, Rianne."

The smile on her face grew wider and she lifted her lashes just a fraction. "I don't want you to."

Leaning in, he bussed her mouth softly. "Stay with me," she whispered.

Carefully, he levered his body onto the narrow bed and she cuddled against him. Eilrah rested his hand on her hip, his thumb rubbing over the satiny flesh.

Her breathing slowed as she drifted back into sleep. Eilrah lowered his head, burying it in the wealth of curls.

Life, he mused, was certainly odd.

He'd thought he had been alive. Just restless. It had been more than that, though. Ever since he had come to be, even as

200

he'd fought to serve his priestess, even as he'd fought to unite Kye and Eiona, he had been waiting.

Waiting for just this.

He hadn't really started to live until this wounded, sad woman had come to him. Before that—he had just existed.

Softly, he repeated, "I won't let you go." Then he sighed, and followed her into sleep.

Also by Shiloh Walker

ജ

A Wish, A Kiss, A Dream *(anthology)*
Back From Hell
Coming In Last
Ellora's Cavemen: Legendary Tails II *(anthology)*
Ellora's Cavemen: Tales From the Temple IV *(anthology)*
Every Last Fantasy
Firewalkers: Dreamer
Firewalkers: Sage
Good Girls Don't
Hearts and Wishes
Her Best Friend's Lover
Her Wildest Dreams
His Christmas Cara
His Every Desire
Hot Spell
Make Me Believe
Myth-behavin' *(anthology)*
Mythe & Magick
Mythe: Vampire
Once Upon a Midnight Blue
One Night with You
One of the Guys
Silk Scarves and Seduction
Telling Tales
The Hunters 1: Delcan and Tori
The Hunters 2: Eli and Sarel
The Hunters 3: Byron and Kit
The Hunters 4: Jonathan and Lori
The Hunters 5: Ben and Shadoe
The Hunters 6: Rafe and Sheila
The Hunters 7: I'll Be Hunting You
Touch of Gypsy Fire
Voyeur
Whipped Cream and Handcuffs

About the Author

෨

Shiloh Walker has been writing since she was a kid. She fell in love with vampires with the book Bunnicula and has worked her way up to the more...ah...serious vampire stories. She loves reading and writing anything paranormal, anything fantasy, but most of all anything romantic. Once upon a time she worked as a nurse, but now she writes full time and lives with her family in the Midwest.

Shiloh welcomes comments from readers. You can find her website and email address on her author bio page at www.ellorascave.com.

Tell Us What You Think

We appreciate hearing reader opinions about our books. You can email us at Comments@EllorasCave.com.

Why an electronic book?

We live in the Information Age — an exciting time in the history of human civilization, in which technology rules supreme and continues to progress in leaps and bounds every minute of every day. For a multitude of reasons, more and more avid literary fans are opting to purchase e-books instead of paper books. The question from those not yet initiated into the world of electronic reading is simply: *Why?*

1. *Price.* An electronic title at Ellora's Cave Publishing and Cerridwen Press runs anywhere from 40% to 75% less than the cover price of the exact same title in paperback format. Why? Basic mathematics and cost. It is less expensive to publish an e-book (no paper and printing, no warehousing and shipping) than it is to publish a paperback, so the savings are passed along to the consumer.

2. *Space.* Running out of room in your house for your books? That is one worry you will never have with electronic books. For a low one-time cost, you can purchase a handheld device specifically designed for e-reading. Many e-readers have large, convenient screens for viewing. Better yet, hundreds of titles can be stored within your new library — on a single microchip. There are a variety of e-readers from different manufacturers. You can also read e-books on your PC or laptop computer. (Please note that Ellora's Cave does not endorse any specific brands. You can check our websites at www.ellorascave.com

or www.cerridwenpress.com for information we make available to new consumers.)

3. *Mobility*. Because your new e-library consists of only a microchip within a small, easily transportable e-reader, your entire cache of books can be taken with you wherever you go.

4. *Personal Viewing Preferences.* Are the words you are currently reading too small? Too large? Too… ANNOYING? Paperback books cannot be modified according to personal preferences, but e-books can.

5. *Instant Gratification.* Is it the middle of the night and all the bookstores near you are closed? Are you tired of waiting days, sometimes weeks, for bookstores to ship the novels you bought? Ellora's Cave Publishing sells instantaneous downloads twenty-four hours a day, seven days a week, every day of the year. Our webstore is never closed. Our e-book delivery system is 100% automated, meaning your order is filled as soon as you pay for it.

Those are a few of the top reasons why electronic books are replacing paperbacks for many avid readers.

As always, Ellora's Cave and Cerridwen Press welcome your questions and comments. We invite you to email us at Comments@ellorascave.com or write to us directly at Ellora's Cave Publishing Inc., 1056 Home Avenue, Akron, OH 44310-3502.

COMING TO A BOOKSTORE NEAR YOU!

ELLORA'S CAVE

Bestselling Authors Tour

UPDATES AVAILABLE AT

WWW.ELLORASCAVE.COM

erridwen, the Celtic Goddess of wisdom, was the muse who brought inspiration to storytellers and those in the creative arts. Cerridwen Press encompasses the best and most innovative stories in all genres of today's fiction. Visit our site and discover the newest titles by talented authors who still get inspired - much like the ancient storytellers did, once upon a time.

Cerridwen Press

www.cerridwenpress.com

Discover for yourself why readers can't get enough of the multiple award-winning publisher Ellora's Cave.

Whether you prefer e-books or paperbacks, be sure to visit EC on the web at www.ellorascave.com

for an erotic reading experience that will leave you breathless.

1489009

Made in the USA